'There's sex  but that's all!'

'It's a business deal,' Faith insisted desperately. 'I want a child, so I need a husband. And you—Max—wanted a wife. You know I can cook, and I promise I'll fulfil the rest of your... of your...'

'My needs? My physical needs?'

She gulped. 'Yes,' she whispered.

'Do I get a sample of the goods?'

She heard the faint squeak of protest from her own throat. 'If... if you want.'

Next month sees a great new look for our Romances—and we can guarantee you'll enjoy our stories just as much. Passionate, sensual, warm and tender—at heart, Mills & Boon Romances are as satisfying as ever.

THE EDITOR

Dear Reader

Over the past year, along with our usual wide variety of exciting romances, you will, we hope, have been enjoying a romantic journey around Europe with our Euromance series. From this month, you'll be able to have double the fun and double the passion, as there will now be two Euromance books each month—one set in one of your favourite European countries, and one on a fascinating European island. Remember to pack your passport!

The Editor

Vanessa Grant began writing her first romance when she was twelve years old. The novel foundered on page fifty, but Vanessa never forgot the magic of having a love-story come to life. Although she went on to become an accountant and a college instructor, she never stopped writing, and in 1985 her first Mills & Boon novel was published. Vanessa and her husband live in a log home in the forest on one of British Columbia's Gulf Islands.

Recent titles by the same author:

AFTER ALL THIS TIME

STRANGERS BY DAY

BY

VANESSA GRANT

MILLS & BOON LIMITED
ETON HOUSE, 18-24 PARADISE ROAD
RICHMOND, SURREY TW9 1SR

For Karin Stoecker
whose suggestion sparked the idea for this story

All the characters in this book have no existence outside the imagination of the Author, and have no relation whatsoever to anyone bearing the same name or names. They are not even distantly inspired by any individual known or unknown to the Author, and all the incidents are pure invention.

All Rights Reserved. The text of this publication or any part thereof may not be reproduced or transmitted in any form or by any means, electronic or mechanical, including photocopying, recording, storage in an information retrieval system, or otherwise, without the written permission of the publisher.

This book is sold subject to the condition that it shall not, by way of trade or otherwise, be lent, resold, hired out or otherwise circulated without the prior consent of the publisher in any form of binding or cover other than that in which it is published and without a similar condition including this condition being imposed on the subsequent purchaser.

*First published in Great Britain 1993
by Mills & Boon Limited*

© Vanessa Grant 1993

*Australian copyright 1993
Philippine copyright 1993
This edition 1993*

ISBN 0 263 78221 2

*Set in Times Roman 10 on 11¼ pt.
01-9309-55383 C*

Made and printed in Great Britain

CHAPTER ONE

FAITH CORSICA caught her breath as the island ahead grew to fill her horizon. Palm trees. White sand, streaks of green water all around.

'Is that it?' she shouted in English.

'*Sí*,' agreed the helicopter pilot. He threw her a perplexed glance.

A week in the States and she was talking English as if it were her only language. No wonder the pilot was confused. He'd naturally assumed from her appearance and her fluent Spanish that she was Latin. Well, so she was—half of her. Her father had been a Corsica, which was as Latin as one could get. It was the American half that kept getting her into trouble. The American that had once eloped with Alan.

The American half that had got her this far today.

It was Cathy who had suggested a week on Isla Catalina. Cathy was the newest in Faith's assortment of Corsica relatives, married to Faith's cousin. Unlike the rest of them, Cathy was American—energetic and modern and rebellious. She had transformed Juan Corsica Perez from an arrogant, proud descendant of the *conquistadores* into a man hopelessly in love with his gringa wife.

'Go to our island,' Cathy had insisted. 'You can have a week. A week with no pressures before you go home.'

Faith had been visiting her cousin Juan and his wife in their San Francisco home—a week of fun stolen before she returned to Peru. Two days before Faith was due to fly out of San Francisco, Juan had left for a business trip to Paris. Alone with Cathy, Faith had found herself confiding her own personal dilemma. Cathy had been outraged at Faith's plans. 'At least stop and think about it for a bit! After all, Faith, if you go through with it, you'll be married a long time. Call it our wedding gift to you. One week. What difference can a week make?'

She had brushed aside Faith's protest of travel reservations made, plans too late to change. 'A few phone calls will put off the Peruvian uncles,' Cathy had insisted. 'And plane reservations are made to be broken.'

So here she was, about to land on a tiny tropical island. Faith tensed as the helicopter tilted, preparing to land. She didn't mind helicopters—not nearly as much as small airplanes, which terrified her. Fifteen minutes' nervousness in a helicopter was nothing when she had such a gift at the other end.

A week, all to herself. Not for thinking. Her decision was already made, but she could use a private, solitary goodbye to whatever dreams of true love had survived the last twelve years.

The pilot flew over palm trees, then over the roof of a single house. No sign of anyone at all—no boat, nobody on the beach. *'Sola?'* he asked her.

'No,' lied Faith. 'I won't be alone.' The pilot was probably in his thirties, a tough-looking small man who had eyed her with Latin speculation from the moment she hired his helicopter back in Mérida. She pointed to her wedding-ring now and said firmly in Spanish, 'My husband is here. Waiting for me.'

The lie sounded like truth.

She was not about to tell him she was alone. She had yet to meet the Latin man who could imagine a woman functioning without the protection of a man. She knew very well that if Juan hadn't flown off to Paris he would never have gone along with his wife's determination to give Faith a week on a tropical island.

Not alone.

As the helicopter touched down, she realised exactly how crazy this was. Alone with the sand and the palms. Alone in the sun, but what if someone came? What if this macho Mexican pilot beside her realised she was lying about the husband? What if he came back tomorrow or the next day, planning to follow up on those speculative glances? She might be a thirty-one-year-old widow, but she hadn't a clue how to handle a situation like that. She'd never managed to graduate to independent American status. Her one attempt at rebellion had ended in disaster. When the helicopter had flown away, would she be alone with the sun and the island, shivering in terror?

Lightly, the helicopter's pontoons settled on to the sand. Faith let out a silent sigh of relief. In time she supposed she might learn to be comfortable in the air, but it hadn't happened yet.

The pilot reached for the box that held her supply of food, then the bag that she'd packed for a week of sun and fun. *'Su esposo?'* he asked, frowning.

Her husband. Where was her husband? She scrambled out of the helicopter, careful to duck down as she had been warned, to avoid the blades. 'He'll be here in a minute. *Momentito*!' She pulled her bag away from him. 'It's OK. You can go.'

He looked uncertain. Suspicious.

Damn! She should have known no Latin man would leave a woman out here alone without questions. 'Next Wednesday,' she said desperately. 'Come back for me next Wednesday.'

Still he hesitated. Waiting for her husband to appear. Waiting to hand her over to a man. Why on earth had she told that crazy lie about a husband? He picked up the box and she realised then that he intended to carry it to the cottage for her.

'No!'

He stopped, staring at her. He must think she was crazy, refusing his help to carry her things. She gestured desperately, her heels sinking into the sand as she turned. 'My husband—*mi esposo*. He'll be hungry.' She repeated that in Spanish, adding, '*Please* leave! *Mi esposo es hombre grande.*' She gestured to indicate a big, angry husband.

The Mexican pilot stopped, clearly uneasy now. Faith tried to look the part of a wife terrified of an overly jealous husband. The pilot looked around when Faith did, then shrugged and turned to go.

'*Adiós, señora! Hasta miércoles.*' Until Wednesday.

Faith lifted her arms to hold down her curly black hair as the helicopter took off. Until Wednesday. She had a week. One week of freedom, then she would go home to Peru. The pilot was going to be certain she was crazy when he came back next week. Again, no husband. Simply a runaway woman returning home.

She supposed this island retreat qualified as the second craziest decision in her life. This time she'd had Cathy as an ally. Last time she'd been alone, unless you counted Alan. She wondered if Juan would be angry with Cathy when he discovered what she'd done. Faith Corsica hadn't much idea what to do if a strange aggressive man should turn up on this sandy beach. Juan would know that. Well, if he was angry, he'd quickly forgive Cathy. Faith believed that Cathy's strong independence was one of the things Juan loved about the woman he'd married.

Cathy would never be nervous in this situation. As Dr Catherine Jenan, the well known archaeological photographer, Juan Corsica's wife was accustomed to living in all sorts of strange places. Cathy had an independence of spirit that Faith had never achieved. She decided glumly that it was probably because she was too much of a coward. If she went swimming here, the sharks might get her. And what if someone came to the island?

Turning slowly, letting her eyes take in the blue sky, the white sand, the swaying palms, Faith realised how sheltered she had been. Ever since her parents had died in Seattle when she was fourteen, she had lived with her father's people. She had become a sheltered Peruvian girl with chaperons.

That summer when she married Alan—well, face it, nothing had really changed. She sucked in a deep breath and turned away from the fading sound of the helicopter heading back to the Mexican mainland. Away from thoughts of Alan.

One week, and damn it! For once she'd be courageous, rash.

A week of sun and surf. A week of independence. No one to answer to.

Solitude.

She tried to remember a time when she'd had more than a day alone. A thirty-one-year-old woman who had never been alone, although there had been years of loneliness. Time she changed that. Seven days of freedom, stolen from fate. What better place for a last fling than the little island Juan had bought for his wife as a wedding present? Isla Catalina, he'd renamed it. For his Catherine, his Catalina. It was a place for loving.

Faith picked up the box and struggled through the sand towards the palms where the cottage was hidden. She was wearing the worst clothes for this—a slim skirt and high heels—fine for the city of Mérida, but crazy on the beach, hot under the sun. She twitched her shoulders as uncomfortable perspiration gathered between her shoulder-blades. Cathy wouldn't put up with high heels and a tight skirt on the beach. Cathy would stop and strip off before she carried stuff up to the cottage.

After all, who would see?

She laughed, the sound startling a bird overhead. It stopped chattering and stared down at Faith. 'Right,' she muttered. 'You and I both know I'd never overcome my inhibitions enough to strip off, no matter how isolated.'

She had spent too many years with disapproving older women watching her every move. Chaperons. Too many years listening to a gasp of shock at her mildest unconventional suggestion. And this last year and a half, running away from it all, look where she'd chosen to run! To Spain to visit a cousin, then working among the nuns, helping in the orphanage. Talk about conformity!

She kicked off her high heels, feeling both reckless and ridiculous. Faith Corsica in rebellion, stockinged feet in the sand. She picked up the heels and dropped them into the box with the food. This was as daring as she was likely to get. Just as well. Recklessness didn't go with being a good Peruvian wife, a fact that had kept Cathy and Juan apart for fourteen years.

Perhaps for those few days alone she would try to pretend she was someone else. How about Faith Corsica going swimming without a stitch of clothing on? She laughed suddenly, thinking of it. Strange and exciting. No one to see.

Maybe after a day or two she'd find the nerve.

She walked between two big palms that shaded her from the hot afternoon sun. Her heart began to race. It *was* a beautiful island. Mexico in April, lazy in the powerful sun. The beach house ahead had a *palapa* roof and a big veranda, the dried palm leaves of the *palapa* rustling in the sea breeze. From the looks of it, there was another beach beyond the grove of palms. Yes, that was the north side of the island. Rockier, but Cathy said it was the place to go swimming. A natural lagoon with no danger of sharks in the shallows.

Sun and sand and a box of food in her arms.

This place was built for sun-worshippers. Juan had bought the island from a Mexican friend who seldom visited it. An island in the Gulf of Mexico was a wild extravagance, a wonderful gift that was only given for one reason: to declare that Juan Corsica Perez loved his wife beyond reason. Faith had just spent a week with the couple. She knew their love was mutual and incredibly powerful. After seeing Cathy and Juan together, it was impossible to imagine them spending their lives apart.

Love. Real love.

Some people were lucky.

There was no lock on the door of the beach house. Under the shade of the *palapa* the sun's power was slightly muted. Faith opened the screen door, balancing the box on one hip. Inside, the sprawling living-room was quietly elegant with thick throw rugs over ceramic-tile floor. Off the living-room, she found a small, complete kitchen.

She put the box on the counter in the kitchen. Ceramic-tile floors here, too, cool under her stockinged feet. Refrigerator, powered by solar cells. Cathy had shrugged about the technicalities. 'The fridge will be cold. That's all you need to worry about.'

Faith opened the cupboard door, automatically beginning to lift tins of food out of the box to put away. In Peru the maid would do this, but during Faith's brief times in the Seattle house with Alan she'd insisted on taking possession of her own kitchen. It made her feel as if it were truly her home.

An illusion.

There was already quite a bit of food in the cupboards. Tins and jars. Stocks left behind when Juan and Cathy were here for a week, back in December. Odd that they'd left the peanut butter here. They must have known it would spoil by the time they returned. She tried to imagine her rather formal cousin eating something that seemed as American as peanut butter. The peanut butter, she decided, must be Cathy's, although Juan would probably eat cardboard if his wife offered it to him. Faith's hand tightened on the jar of peanut butter, thinking of her cousin and the love he and his wife shared.

Thinking of herself and what was ahead.

The wedding... the wedding night.

No. Best not to think of that.

She turned abruptly, leaving the cupboard doors open, the box half full of food. The food was mostly tins, except for the tortillas. No harm in leaving it.

She was going for a swim.

'Spoil yourself a bit,' Cathy had ordered. 'Forget who you are, all the things you feel you have to do. Just go to our island and relax for a week. Swim and sun and enjoy, and if you still want to marry Jorge Sulca Mendez afterwards——' Cathy had shrugged '—at least give yourself a week to consider.'

She'd already had a year to consider. A year since the traditional period of mourning was over. A year of avoiding the inevitable. She could have stayed in Spain, but in the end she had known that it was time to get on with her life. Time to go back. Time to marry again. Unless she wanted to join the ranks of the chaperons, she had to marry.

This time she would make her own terms. She would insist. It would be...well, a business deal. That was how Jorge saw it, and he was Latin enough in any case to be certain to want children. Not like Alan.

She would be realistic this time. She was no longer a young innocent of nineteen, disillusioned when she realised she'd been married for her family connections. She knew the score now. This time she would negotiate her own terms. Children. Babies. She blinked back the dampness threatening in her eyes. Damn! She was not going to cry! That was the worst of the Latin part of her heritage. Easy tears, emotions threatening too close to the surface. She had cried enough two years ago. There was no way she could undo the tragedies of the past.

Hot! Even here in the cottage, in the heat of an April afternoon, it was hot. Siesta time, but she was filled with uneasy restlessness. She bent to pull off her stockings, stuffed them into her box of food, and padded, barefoot, across the kitchen floor to the stairway while she undid the buttons of her blouse. She felt a crawling in the flesh at her back, as if she were watched—bare legs and bare feet, her blouse undone.

This was a holiday home. She was alone except for the sea-birds and the dolphins and whales Cathy had told her to look for. There was no chaperon to tell her that a swim in the ocean would ruin her make-up. Nobody at all to see. Faith hummed slightly, going up the stairs, pulling her blouse off as she came to the first door.

'Use the big bedroom, the first one upstairs,' Cathy had instructed. 'It's got a beautiful big balcony; it's gorgeous at night, sitting out there with the ocean breezes blowing over you.'

Faith dropped her blouse on the bed and unfastened the button at the waist of her skirt. The bed was made up. She thought Cathy had said the bedding was kept in sealed plastic bags in the cupboard at the end of the corridor, but here the bed was, neatly made and waiting for her. Had Cathy arranged for someone to come out here and prepare the place for her? It seemed unlikely. It was only two days since they'd made the arrangements, sitting in the living-room in San Francisco overlooking the bay, Cathy confessing that even a weekend apart from Juan left her yearning to grab a jet and join him in Paris.

'Why don't you?' Faith had asked. 'I'll be leaving, going to your island.'

'I wish I could. I'm due at a dig in Brazil on Friday. Jack's joining me there in about ten days.' It always startled Faith to hear Cathy call her very Peruvian cousin Jack. A name no one but Cathy ever used for Juan Corsica. When Faith had asked about it, Cathy had laughed and said he'd been Jack to her ever since she was a teenage girl visiting Peru with her archaeologist father.

Faith stepped out of her skirt and tossed it on top of her blouse in a jumble. Her bathing-suit was outside with the suitcase. She looked down the length of her body. Lacy bra. Bikini panties. She smiled slightly. Why not? When she got to the water, she might even take these two scraps off. She'd never in her life swum naked, but there was no reason for modesty *here*. Why not take a memory of a little adventure back with her?

No one would ever know.

Towels, as Cathy had said, were in the cupboard in the corridor. Faith picked up a fluffy pink towel, swinging it from her hand as she padded down the wooden stairs in bare feet. Clean white sand outside. No need to dig for the sandals she had brought. She went through the door to the veranda, careful to close the screen behind her to keep any flying insects outside. She felt the heat of the sand under her feet. Glorious! She looked both ways, but there was no one here. Of course not!

She would make it a short swim. With that sun pounding down, she could get burned in minutes. Her skin was fair despite the darkness of her long, curly hair. Fair skin, the legacy of her gringa mother. She rounded the stand of palm trees, hurrying, almost running, feeling the sand clean and gritty under her bare feet.

Then she froze.

Her fingers clenched into the softness of the towel hanging from her left hand.

A man. A man walking up the slope from the rocks! Almost naked.

He looked like a mountain, coming towards her. Tall and broad and covered with sun-bronzed skin and beads of sea water. Faith gulped and gripped the towel with nerveless fingers. She tried to say something. What? She felt a scream crawling up her throat. He kept coming closer.

Who was he? What was he doing here? She tried to step back, to run, but her legs were frozen. The island, a few palm trees and a palm-covered holiday home, the helicopter pilot long gone now, and herself alone on the beach with a man who kept coming closer.

A big man. Too big.

He stopped only a metre away from her. There were two deep lines carved into his face beside his mouth. Little lines near his eyes. Lines of character, of laughter. And muscles. His chest. His shoulders. The flat abdomen that led to...

He wasn't just tall. He was *big* in every way. Muscles. Hard muscles everywhere. No softness anywhere on him. Her eyes dropped in horrified fascination to the scrap of his swimming-trunks. Then she realised where she was staring and jerked her gaze back to his face.

He was glowering at her. She thought wildly of the nervous fantasies she'd suppressed only moments ago. She'd pushed away the image of being ravished here on this island by a big stranger. Nonsense. Of course it was nonsense!

The way he was staring at her, he was more likely to strangle her than rape her.

She saw his gaze shift from her face to her body on to her bra, a lacy thing that felt pretty, but had never been meant to be seen. And her panties...! She pulled the towel tightly against her, but it didn't cover, and she could feel his dark brown eyes invading as he stared at the pushed-up curves of her breasts...the flat curve of her belly above her panties...the length of her naked legs.

Who in God's name was he?

What was going to happen?

She pulled at the towel again, trying to spread it over her nakedness, but it wasn't as big as she'd thought. It was thick, but it only half covered the places he was looking at. It was only a hand-towel, and she needed a big beach-towel desperately!

If only she had Cathy's casual confidence! Cathy would say something sharp and discouraging. She'd get covered somehow and tell this half-naked specimen of manhood to get off her island and stay off!

He was carrying a spear gun in one hand, goggles for swimming underwater in the other. When he spoke, his voice came harsh and unfriendly. 'Who the hell are you? What the devil are you doing here? *Qué*...?' He shrugged away the effort to think up the words to put his question in Spanish. He was a gringo, uncomfortable with Spanish.

She swallowed a dry lump of fear. 'I'm... Who are you?' He was the stranger. Cathy would tell him so pretty quickly if she were here. Faith swallowed and clenched her hands more tightly into the towel. 'This island is private property!' The words came out quavering.

'Yes,' he said slowly, his voice deep and rhythmic with a lazy accent she could not place. Something had changed in his eyes. 'Of course it's private property. I'm Max Davidson. I'm a guest here.'

'A guest?' Faith saw the shift of his eyes to her face. She realised that she was chewing nervously on her lower lip.

'Don't you have any clothes?' he asked abruptly, his eyes frozen on her hand where it clutched the towel to her breasts.

She flushed.

'Put them on, would you?'

A boat. He must be off a boat anchored somewhere near the island. But he'd said he was... a guest. 'Whose guest? Who invited you here?'

His brows lifted, dark brows that were thick and sharply defined. 'I might ask the same of you. The owners invited me to spend a couple of weeks.'

'They—they know you're here?' Faith gulped.

'They knew I was coming.' His eyes returned to the place where the towel failed to cover the swelling that was her breast, then moved down to the lacy edge of her panties on her hip. She shifted her leg uneasily. As if he had touched there. She felt the uncomfortable thickening in her bloodstream as his eyes slowly took inventory of her nakedness.

'And you?' he demanded softly. 'I assume you're not alone? Who invited you?' The suspicion, unfriendly and dark, was back in his voice now. 'Two weeks of sun and solitude—that's what Juan offered me—so I doubt that you and your friend...' His eyes must have caught her wedding-ring, because he broke off and changed that to, 'I doubt you and your husband are here by invitation.'

'Juan invited you?'

He nodded and shifted the spear gun in his hand. Planning to shoot her with it, she thought wildly.

'And Cathy? Does she know you're here?'

He inclined his head, indicating wordlessly that it was her turn to explain herself.

Cathy had sent Faith here. Cathy, who had declared hotly only two days ago that Faith must not let grief drive her to marry a man she did not love. Cathy, who must have known Max Davidson was here on the island. She had been set up.

CHAPTER TWO

FAITH lifted her hand to push back her hair, then clutched wildly when the towel began to slip. He was waiting for her to answer his question.

'I...'

'It *is* a private island.' His quiet voice only emphasised his size. A big man. Dangerous, despite the soft voice. His eyes surveyed her boldly. 'Lady, I don't give a damn if you've got gorgeous skin and sexy curves. If you're trespassing I want you off this island.' His eyes narrowed. 'How did you come? Are you off a yacht?'

'I... by helicopter.'

'Helicopter? I did hear a chopper fly over, but I must have been underwater when it landed or I'd have... What are you doing here?'

She took a deep breath, let it go suddenly when his eyes fixed on the expansion of her chest. *Why* had she been so crazy as to come out here in her briefest underwear? She yanked the towel up, then realised that she'd uncovered her skimpy bikini panties. 'I'm Juan Corsica's cousin,' she muttered.

'Cousin? You speak English as if...' She saw that he believed her. She could see him taking in her dark curls, dark eyes. He'd thought she was American because she'd been speaking English, but he could see she was Latin when he looked. He could see entirely too much of her! Too much skin. Hers. And his.

In Peru, a woman seldom saw a man's naked chest. What was commonplace in the States was immodest in Peru. Faith tried not to look, but her gaze kept following the curves of his muscles, iron-hard and sun-bronzed.

'Juan and Cathy told me I could—er—use the island for a holiday.' She flushed at the lie. Juan would never have sent her here when there was no one in sight. Only this man. 'You're not...not alone here?'

He frowned again and she fought the strangest impulse to reach out and smooth his frown.

'Juan knew I wanted to be alone,' he said grimly. 'A fact that makes me sceptical of your story.'

'Story?' She knew she was blushing, thinking of Cathy and what must be a bit of matchmaking. 'I didn't realise there was anyone here.' Had Cathy really planned to throw her at this man? She swallowed, her voice slightly hoarse as she explained desperately, 'I've just come back from a year and a half in Spain. I'm on my way home to—to Peru.' She blinked, shaken by the uneasy feeling that he knew she wasn't telling the whole truth. The truth, but so much left out. 'I thought I'd stop for a few days, have a rest before I went home. Juan...' With those eyes on her, she could not tell a lie. She bit her lip. 'I didn't think that...'

He pushed back wet hair with his free hand. Faith found her eyes following the ripple of muscles in his upper arm. 'Your husband?' he demanded. 'Where is he?'

She stared down at her wedding-ring. 'I'm...alone.'

'Alone?' She saw him swallow, saw the motion jerk through his throat. His head swung around, looking towards the palms that concealed the beach house. 'Your clothes?'

'I—I should get dressed.'

'Yes,' he snapped. The lines were harsh on his face, telling her the last thing she had to worry about from him was sexual advances. He had certainly looked at her, had made her skin flush with uncomfortable awareness, but he wasn't pleased that she was alone, without male protection.

'I'll—I'll go and...'

She couldn't seem to move. If only he would stop watching her like that. If only he would turn away, she could run back to the house. With his eyes on her, every muscle in her body seemed frozen, although her nerves were crawling with uneasiness. She could see the drops of sea water drying rapidly on his chest, the tangle of his chest hair curling as the sun sucked moisture out of it. Her fingers were cramped, curled in on themselves, and she felt the pressure of some great weight on her lungs, making breathing difficult and loud enough that she feared he would hear. The sun was hot on her face, on the naked flesh above her bra.

'Could you..turn away?' she begged. 'Could you not— not watch me like that?'

He turned without a word and walked down the beach, towards the water. Even then, staring at his back, it took an effort for her to move. Then she ran, bare feet pounding on the sand as she fled into the shelter of the palms, up the three steps to the big, shaded patio, through the screen door. It slammed behind her. Up the stairs into the bedroom. The bedroom with the neatly made bed, her clothes strewn on top.

She shut the door, heard her own breath loud on the stillness of the afternoon. The breeze had stopped. The ocean had ceased its murmur on the sand. Quiet. Heavy. Hot. Crazy fool, going out dressed like that!

She had thought she was completely alone. Safe.

She picked up her blouse and buttoned it over her bra, then had to do it again because she had one button left over at the bottom. Her stockings... no, she'd stripped off her stockings downstairs and pushed them into the corner of the box of food. If he came into the house and looked in that box...

He was a gringo, not Peruvian. A pair of women's stockings would mean nothing to him. The way he'd looked at her, his eyes stripping away even that towel... She shuddered. There had been curiosity in his gaze, and awareness. But even though she'd been nearly naked, Max Davidson had been cold enough to be angry at her presence, to resent her invading his privacy.

She pulled her skirt on, wishing for something less feminine than the city clothes she'd worn for the helicopter trip. She had borrowed jeans from Cathy yesterday, but they were in her bag near where the helicopter had landed. She hadn't brought the bag inside yet. She had carried the box of food to the kitchen, then succumbed to the urge for a swim.

She smoothed her skirt, walking slowly to the mirror over the big vanity unit. This room must be where Cathy and Juan slept when they came to the island. This mirror... Faith closed her eyes and she could imagine them here. Cathy at the mirror, brushing her short blonde hair, watching Juan through the mirror as he came up behind her, his darkness a contrast to Cathy's fair femininity as he bent to kiss her throat.

She had to stop this! Had to stop yearning for something she couldn't have. That week with Cathy and Juan had been a mistake. Watching their happiness, seeing the barely perceptible swelling of Cathy's belly and guessing about the coming baby even before Cathy confided...

Cathy and Juan deserved their happiness. It was terrible for Faith to be jealous of what they'd found with each other, to wish it were herself. There was a hairbrush on the dresser. She picked it up and dragged it through her long curls. She wished she had her combs to make her hair more tidy—the combs Alan had given her, combs to trap the wildness of her curls. She didn't want to go downstairs, to face that man. Not when she was like this, her hair all wild and her cheeks flushed from the sun. She pulled the brush through again, but the bristles weren't penetrating the thick mass of her hair.

It was a man's brush.

She turned slowly to stare at the bed. There was a book on the bedside table. She approached it slowly, warily, and it was a spy thriller. Did Juan read spy thrillers? If so, he probably bought them in Spanish. Beside it was another book, a Spanish-English dictionary. There was no reason on earth why either Juan or Cathy would need that dictionary.

It was his.

She pulled the covers to straighten the slight crease she'd put there. He was sleeping in this room. Max Davidson. She went to the wardrobe and there were trousers and a white cotton shirt on one hanger, a brown blazer hanging on another. She touched the blazer and it had to be his too, because it was far too large for Juan, and in any case that casual blazer wasn't the sort of thing Juan Corsica would wear. Too informal.

She backed away from the wardrobe.

His bedroom. She had to get out of here!

She went down the stairs slowly, warily approaching the sounds she could hear from the kitchen. She was very aware of her bare feet. Her shoes and stockings were in the box in the kitchen. Had he rummaged through the box? She didn't want to face him in bare feet, but confronting Max Davidson was the first step to getting out of here. He would have a way to leave. She couldn't swim, but there would be a radio somewhere. Cathy had mentioned a radio.

As she came through the door to the kitchen he turned. He was still wearing only the brief black swimming trunks, but he was dry now. His wet hair had resolved into sandy brown, lighter than his eyes and drying into unruly waves.

'Much better.' He swept her rose silk blouse and matching skirt with his swift gaze. 'Your beach clothes?'

She flushed at the irony in his voice. He seemed completely unconscious of the fact that he was dressed in almost nothing himself, but when his gaze lingered on her bare feet she shifted uncomfortably.

'My bag is still down on the beach.' She gestured. 'Where the helicopter landed. Are you planning to attack me with that knife? If not, I wish you'd put it down.'

He glanced down at the long, evil knife in his hand. A slow smile curved his lips, deepening the creases on either side of his mouth. 'Cleaning fish,' he explained, pointing the knife towards the sink, where she could see a partially dismembered fish. 'What's your name?'

'Faith.'

His brows went up. 'Doesn't sound very Peruvian to me.'

'My mother was an American.' She realised that her hands were clenched together and forced them to relax.

'Where's your husband? He must be American too. I can't see a Latin man letting his woman come out here on her own.'

'Letting?' The protest was mechanical. Crazy, when she'd been a good Latin girl for so many years. Just that one wild protest—eloping with Alan when she was nineteen.

He laughed. 'So he *is* American. Where is he?'

She didn't want to tell him. A husband seemed like a good invention, protection in case Max Davidson developed ideas.

'Is he joining you here?'

'He...no.'

'Are you frightened of me?' He looked down at the knife in his hands, and laughed shortly. 'This is for the fish. I'm not a wild murderer, just an overworked Canadian rancher.'

That explained the muscles. 'Is that how you know Juan? From ranching?'

'That's right.' He leaned back against the counter, the knife still in his hands, his legs long and well muscled. 'Juan owns the ranch next to mine.'

'You're from British Columbia?' She knew Juan had a cattle-breeding ranch there.

'Hmm. And you? Peru, or the States with your American husband?'

'I...' At the moment she had no home. The Lima *casa* she had lived in with Alan had been sold, along with the highly mortgaged Seattle house. She saw the impatience in his eyes. He must think she was unable to answer the simplest question.

'I've been living in Spain, visiting really,' she explained. 'I'm on my way back to Peru, so——' she shrugged '—I suppose you could say I'm from Peru.'

'Your husband isn't with you?'

'No. I... He...'

'Where is he?'

'Alan died two years ago.'

'I'm sorry.' He stared down at the knife in his hand and she had no idea what he was thinking. When he looked up, his eyes were quiet and dark. 'One of us has to leave, you know.'

'Yes, I know. I will.' Gladly. She'd been insane to think she could behave as Cathy might. Juan's wife might have spent her life getting away with wild impulses, but Faith had known for years that going against the rules never worked for her. And the rules were completely clear in this case. A good Peruvian widow should be heading directly home to her relatives, not taking a detour and a week's escape.

'When?' he demanded.

'When?' she echoed. 'When what?'

He pushed back an unruly lock of sandy hair with an impatient gesture. 'I don't want to seem inhospitable. It's not my island. But I know enough about Juan's culture to know he wouldn't want us both to be here together. Alone.'

'I...no.' Cathy had had no such inhibition. How could Cathy *do* this to her? 'I...if you could get me a helicopter? On the radio? I'll go as soon as it can get here. Is...there *is* a radio, isn't there?'

'Yes.' He turned back to the sink and she heard the clatter of his knife. His voice was slightly muffled. 'A broken radio.'

It had to be a cruel joke. This couldn't really be happening to her! She whispered, 'My helicopter's coming back next Wednesday.'

He muttered a curse.

'You're sure about the radio?' she asked desperately.

'I'll try it again, but it's not working.'

'Surely Juan wouldn't be out here with only one radio?'

Max shrugged. 'Juan and Cathy normally bring a small seaplane when they come. It's got a radio. I chartered a plane out, and like your helicopter, it's——' he shrugged shoulders that were impossibly broad '—it's gone.'

He walked past her, making her feel crowded, so that she backed up to give him extra room. The radio was at the end of the kitchen counter. She stared at him as he picked up the microphone and spoke into it. He tried calling several times, on several channels, then shrugged. 'See? It's had it.' She knew nothing about radios, but he obviously did.

'I already checked the battery leads and the aerial connection,' he said as he hung up the microphone. 'They're fine. Whatever's gone is in its innards.' His lips turned down. 'I did open it up and take a look, but it needs a proper technician and test equipment.'

She turned away and walked into the living-room, over to the window where she could look out and see water. The ocean. She heard sounds behind her. His footsteps, bare feet on the tiles.

'You won't find any boats stopping here, Faith.' She closed her eyes and she could see him too clearly as he spoke. 'There are underwater rocks all around, hazardous waters for any boat larger than a Mexican fisherman's *panga*.'

She swung around to face him. 'A fisherman might come.' He was tall, very tall. She wished she had her high heels on. Anything to diminish this feeling of vulnerability. She thought of Cathy, who had given her a hug in the waiting-room of the San Francisco airport. What in God's name had Cathy thought would happen here? Did she think Faith and this man would fall in love with each other on first sight?

'Not likely,' he said.

Had she been speaking her thoughts aloud? She gulped and shoved her hand through her curls. Her fingers tangled in the unruly confusion she had been unable to tame with his brush. 'What's not likely?' she demanded frantically.

'A fisherman.' He was looking at her as if she were losing her mind. 'I was talking to the pilot who brought me—to the extent that we could communicate with my Spanish. He said the fishermen tend to operate closer in to the mainland. There's a tricky current to the south of this island. The local fishermen avoid it.'

How could Cathy have *done* this to her?

'We're stuck here, I'm afraid.'

'Give me two weeks and no woman in miles. I'd give my eye-teeth for that.'

Five months ago, when Max Davidson had ground out those angry words, he had been in his corral with Juan Corsica, examining a bullock he'd bought from Juan's breeding ranch only the week before.

'Seems better,' Max decided after examining the animal thoroughly. 'You've had no sign of anything in your stock?'

'No. Nothing.' Juan was frowning at the bull. Max knew he was thinking of the danger of a contagious virus in cattle. 'Those blood samples from my stock were processed in the lab in Calgary yesterday. Clear, they say.'

Max nodded. 'This one too. I got word last night. I guess we're OK.'

'Está bien.'

'Coffee?' offered Max. 'I've got a Thermos up at the house.'

'Sounds good,' agreed Juan politely, although Max knew that the Peruvian only tolerated his neighbour's coffee out of politeness.

'By the way,' Max announced with practiced casualness, 'the wedding's off.'

Juan said nothing until Max joined him at the gate. 'I have heard rumours.'

Max grimaced. 'Word does get around.'

'It is definite, then?'

'Oh, yes. There won't be a reconciliation. You don't seem surprised?' He saw something in the Peruvian's eyes and asked, 'Why not?' Everyone in the district had been pleased that Max Davidson was finally about to tie the knot. Juan had congratulated both Max and Alice with a formal courtesy that gave nothing of his feelings away.

'Catalina,' Juan said, his voice softening as it always did when he referred to his wife. 'She said it wouldn't work between you and Alice. And in any case...' Juan shrugged, leaving Max wondering what his friend had been about to say. 'Can I do anything?'

'Give me two weeks without a woman within miles. Every single woman in the area seems to have the urge to console me.'

Juan's laughter was sudden, hearty on the cold morning. 'I can give you that. When would you like your two weeks to start?'

Originally, he planned to get free of the ranch after Christmas, but his foreman's mother died and Max couldn't leave. By the time Hank was back on the job, it didn't seem that important to get away. He realised that he was not meant for marriage, for sharing his home or his life. He'd been a bit crazy this last year, watching his sister Beth and her family, realising what he'd been missing all these years. He'd been working too hard until now, struggling to get the ranch into the black after the mess his father had left.

With the ranch a firm success, and a respectable portfolio of investments to insure against a bad year, Max had started dreaming of coming in after a hard day to find the kitchen warm and scented with the aromas that seemed a special woman's magic. Food prepared with love and joy, his woman waiting with a smile, with softness and love. The kids tearing into the kitchen, shouting and laughing and demanding to know if supper was ready yet.

Then he'd run into Alice while he was getting supplies in Williams Lake. She was back in the area after three years in Vancouver. He remembered Alice from years back, but now she seemed soft and blonde and willing.

For a while, he'd gone a bit mad.

He'd come to his senses quickly enough when he'd overheard her with her lover. She wouldn't marry Tom Jergins. No, Tom was too poor, and why should she take on a life of poverty when she could have one of the richest ranchers in the area? Max had been frozen, listening to the conversation he'd almost walked in on. He had heard enough, but before he could escape he'd had the privilege of hearing his fianceé promise her lover that the marriage needn't make any difference to them. As long as they were careful, they could still meet.

He and Alice hadn't promised each other undying love, but he had expected the same loyalty from her that he was prepared to give.

The gossip occasioned by the cancelled wedding died down by Christmas. There was the annual party at the Dentons to talk about, and the fact that Cindy Horrerton was going to have a baby, the speculation over who the father was. Then Charlie Topper's barn burned down and there was no one left to worry about whether Max and Alice would make up.

One way and another, it was the first of April before Max took Juan Corsica up on his offer of a tropical island. By the time he actually got to Isla Catalina, he knew he'd been lucky to escape matrimony with Alice.

He loved Isla Catalina from the beginning. It had been a long time since he had spent four days alone, swimming and fishing and not worrying about anything at all. Not since his father's death. Before that, he'd been a veterinary surgeon in Williams Lake, and he'd had time for hunting and fishing trips into the wilds.

Isla Catalina reminded him of those trips. Not that it was rough or wild, but he had the same sense of being alone with nature, of complete peace. He didn't bother dressing at all, spent the whole day in swimming-trunks, amused at himself because he was enjoying playing Robinson Crusoe. Two weeks of it and he'd probably be itching to get back to the ranch, but the sun and the lazy afternoon breeze made it easy to understand why tropical islands were regarded as a little taste of paradise.

Until he walked out of the sea and saw the woman.

At first, he thought he'd imagined her. It seemed the most likely explanation. He had been among the rocks, diving underwater, telling himself he was spear fishing, but mostly he'd been studying the coral formations underwater. He'd heard the helicopter overhead when he came up once, but he had gone underwater again. He had good lungs, could stay underwater a long time. He made several more dives before he tired, then he swam, respecting the boundaries of the lagoon because of the possibility of sharks outside.

Refreshed, he dived again, this time hunting for his supper. He got a small yellow-fin and dropped it on the sand at the edge of the water. Then he saw her. A woman on the beach. She was all generous dark hair and naked flesh. If he were to fantasise a lover to share this tropical paradise, she would be that woman.

His heart stopped. She was walking towards him.

She was wearing two scraps of creamy lace. He could see the fullness of her breasts above the bra. The panties below were brief, enough to stop a man's heart, to send his hand reaching, needing to know what was hidden. These two scraps of clothing were more seductive than total nakedness could ever have been.

He'd never seen such incredible hair. It was black. Pure, abundant black. Rioting with curls, cascading down over her shoulders, stopping short of the creamy curves of her breasts. She stopped, frozen, a sculptor's vision of passion and beauty.

He moved closer, memorising her with his eyes as he was drawn up the beach. Her flesh was soft, pale except for the colour that flowed in her cheeks, in the soft curves about that scrap of lace. A towel in her hand, just a scrap. When she moved to cover herself with it, he felt the shock of her. Her eyes were wide and deep, black as the curls flowing over her shoulders.

She was real!

Then he saw the wedding-ring, and he was swamped with regret.

He wanted her.

She belonged to another man.

Was he insane? She was a stranger, a vision turned real.

When he finally got her to retreat to the house, the irrational pull she had for him did not go away. When she returned from upstairs, he had a hell of a time keeping his eyes from reminding her that he knew what was under the blouse, under the skirt.

She was standing at the living-room window now, facing away from him. Trapped on this island with him. Her silk blouse was covering the creamy softness he knew was underneath. When she turned to look at him, he had to suppress his reaction. Well covered, except that her legs were bare, and her feet. Bare feet, and he could not stop himself staring at them, because he could still see her as she had been on the beach. A creature made for passion, hurrying towards him on the sand, covered only with scraps to inflame a man.

Now that she was dressed, he could see that she was exactly what she claimed to be. Juan Corsica's cousin, an upper-class Peruvian woman, accustomed to convention and covered flesh. He could see the awareness in her eyes, the uncomfortable knowledge that he had seen what was beneath the silk, that she had stood before him as a woman might stand before the man she loved.

'I'm going to get my bag,' she said stiffly.

'I'll get it.' He dragged his gaze away from her bare feet. He didn't smile with the offer, but he could guess at the kind of life she led. She wasn't accustomed to carrying bags for herself. 'Why in God's name did you come out here alone?' he demanded. Trapped on an island with a beautiful woman. It sounded like every man's dream. What in God's name was he going to do with her?

The heat crawled up her face. When she bit her lower lip, he saw her teeth press into the softness. She was wearing lipstick, some sort of coral that caught the flush of her cheeks and echoed it. He had to clear his throat before he could talk.

'Where's your bag? Which side of the island?'

She gestured, started to protest, but he didn't listen. He had to get away from her. How the hell did a man get away from a woman when they were alone except for thirty-four palm trees and one house with a big veranda and two bedrooms upstairs?

Bedrooms.

With her sleeping in the next room, he'd have to be dead to get a good night's sleep. God! A week until her chopper came back. What if nothing came to rescue him before that week was up? Just how was he going to get through seven days without reaching for her?

He could try reducing her to skin and bones. He was a vet, and he'd studied some human anatomy along with learning about cows and dogs. If he could think of her as just skin and bones... skin and bones and curves arranged to attract the male of the species. The world was full of beautiful women. Four days on a tropical island had obviously taken its toll of his sanity if he saw one woman endowed with sultry creamy curves and could not make himself stop wanting to...

He should be able to look at her and see... his sister. Yes. Beth was a good-looking woman. He would pretend she was Beth. Widowed or not, the lady was not his to pursue. She was Juan Corsica's cousin, and Juan would expect him to behave like a gentleman.

It was just hormones, or perhaps five months of abstinence finally taking its toll. Nothing he couldn't handle.

CHAPTER THREE

FAITH heard Max Davidson come in while she was still in the bathroom, heard his tread going upstairs. She came silently out of the bathroom into the kitchen. Her heels made too much noise on the ceramic floor tiles. He must be able to hear. She continued unpacking the box. It seemed the only thing to do. Either that or swim for the shore of Mexico. She felt a little better now that she had her heels and stockings back on.

She put a jar of preserves beside his peanut butter. That jar of peanut butter should have been a give-away that someone was on the island. That and the fact that the bed upstairs was completely made. She should have realised, should have kept her clothes on.

He was coming back down the stairs now! She wished she had a little more of the casual American in her. A lot more! Cathy would think nothing of it. Cathy must have shared accommodation with lots of men at archaeological digs. It didn't mean anything. There were two bedrooms upstairs and...

She held her breath when he came into the kitchen. She had planned to be looking at the box, not at him, but he caught her staring. He paused, returning her look with impatience in his own eyes. His gaze travelled down. Her stockings. The high heels. And she could read his mind. A sandy island in the sun, and she was dressed for city streets, all her armour on.

He was wearing only those trunks. They were plain, black and too brief for comfort. He broke their locked gaze crossed the floor in bare feet, and went to the sink, where the fish had been reduced to two clean fillets.

'I put your bag in the second bedroom upstairs.' He threw her an inscrutable glance over his shoulder. 'Why don't you go up and get into something more comfortable?'

She had an immediate and graphic image of an old American movie, of the sultry heroine bringing the hero to her home, then offering to get into something more comfortable.

The prelude to love.

She cleared her throat. He wasn't looking at her. He was doing something to those fillets. This had never happened to her before, high-voltage fields around a stranger. She didn't like it. She sucked in a deep breath of sea air. 'I think we should pretend we're—guests at the same hotel.'

He said nothing.

'Strangers,' she added.

'All right.' He did not even look up.

He must be a man accustomed to hiding his thoughts. Not a passionate Latin. A cold northerner. It was easier to be strangers trapped here with a gringo than with a Latin man. A Peruvian wouldn't be able to keep the awareness of the man-woman thing out of his eyes or his voice. Face it, if she were here alone with a Peruvian, it would mean...a good Peruvian girl simply *wouldn't*!

He put the fillets on to a plate. 'Does being strangers include sharing meals?' he asked.

'I...whatever you prefer, I can...cook if you want.' She tossed her hair back uncomfortably, wishing she could hide from the amusement in his eyes, from that slight smile on his face.

'Can you?' He was sceptical. 'Why don't you go take that swim I interrupted?'

'I thought—I didn't think there was anyone else here.'

'I know that.' His voice gentled. 'Go swim. I'll cook the fish.'

She shook her head. 'I can cook the supper.'

'I'd bet that I'm more accustomed to a kitchen than you. I'll do it.'

'I *can* cook,' she muttered.

What did it matter if he thought she was one of the *gente dorada*? Wasn't that what she would be when she married Jorge? A leisured member of the idle wealthy—the fate her uncles wished for her. A woman who looked to the maid when mealtimes came. 'I'll cook,' she repeated doggedly.

'No, thanks.' His voice was harsh. 'Go have your swim. This time, wear a suit.'

She fled upstairs to the second bedroom. Cathy might be the sort to stay and fight it out, but Faith knew she didn't have it in her. His words echoed in her ears. '*This time, wear a suit.*' As if she'd been—been *flaunting* herself for him!

She unpacked quickly, angrily. Jeans and shorts in the dresser, drawers shoved closed with a bang. She threw her black bathing-suit on the bed. She felt sticky and hot. Angry. Furious. A swim—what if he came down to watch? She'd been swimming on public beaches before, had worn this very suit without any self-consciousness. It was a modest suit, a black one-piece.

The last thing he wanted was to watch her. '*This time, wear a suit.*'

Faith pulled on the suit, then hung her blouse and skirt in the wardrobe. When she closed the wardrobe door, the mirror on the door swung to face her. She gasped. Anyone who looked would have no doubt of the shape of her. She remembered how she had felt standing on that beach in almost nothing, his eyes on her.

What was she doing here?

Why hadn't she laughed Cathy's crazy suggestion away?

She belonged back in Peru, safely under the protection of the Corsica men.

She sank down on to the bed. She'd never been alone like this. Lord, she hadn't ever been so alone... even in her marriage. No one for miles. And, in her mind, awareness of all the things a man and woman might do together. He didn't want her here, and she certainly didn't *want* to be here! But... She smoothed her hands down the curves moulded by the black bathing-suit and wondered if she could stay up in this bedroom for a week, lock the door and hide.

She rushed over to the door, gripped the knob. No lock! She had no lock on her bedroom door! And she was thinking of going down there in her bathing-suit!

His smile would turn to laughter if he had any idea how terrified she was.

She turned back to the mirror. This was the same bathing-suit she'd bought three years ago when she'd been on that disastrous California trip with Alan. Modest. Alan had scoffed at her modesty. But the man downstairs...

On the beach he had studied her thoroughly. Her face flamed, as if his eyes were on her again. She liked to wear lacy lingerie. Silk and satin made her feel like a woman, although it was only for herself and she kept it hidden. Not today! There had been nothing but lace and skin, and Max Davidson had been very aware of her as a woman down on that beach. She gulped and told herself that he could obviously turn it off when he wanted. Awareness or not, he had not been happy to find her on what he plainly regarded as *his* beach.

Seven days on an island. If it had been a hotel, she would have no problem ignoring the big man with the unruly brown hair. She could walk past him in her bathing-suit and pretend he was not there. In a hotel, the fact that he was sleeping in the next room would mean nothing.

In a hotel, there would be a lock on the door!

She picked up a towel before she left the bedroom. A very large towel! She closed the door behind her, as if it really *were* a hotel. Her bare feet were silent on the stairs, no warning clatter of high heels. Halfway down the stairs, she caught a glimpse of a naked bronzed back through the kitchen door and her heart stopped. She froze, staring at him, knowing her suit wasn't nearly modest enough and he'd turn and then she'd be trapped again, locked in his cold gaze.

Or the heated gaze from down on the beach.

He moved. Her hand clenched on the banister.

Then he was gone. She could see only the kitchen cabinets through the open doorway. She heard the sound of pans clattering and softly, like a child escaping supervision, she slipped down the stairs and out of the front door.

No problem. Both the American and the Peruvian half of Faith Corsica knew how to ignore strange men in hotels. She breathed more easily as she went through the trees and down to the beach. You couldn't see this part of the beach from the house.

She began to run towards the water.

She ran straight in, not letting herself be tempted by the rock that looked perfect for diving. She didn't know these waters and she was not about to injure herself. She would be dependent on *him* for rescue.

She suspected that he would be good at coming to the rescue.

The water was up to her thighs, soothing the heat of the day with gentle warmth, tempting her further. Cathy had said this was the best place to swim, sandy underfoot, but there were rocks and coral formations all around to form a small lagoon—protection from any sharks that might be in the area.

Her hair streamed out behind her when she began to swim. She took a breath and dived down, swimming underwater, feeling the pleasant drag from her long hair. After a day spent in airports and flying machines this water was a sensual delight.

Would he put on clothes for dinner? Could she possibly eat her food if she had to stare across the table at that naked broad chest? She surfaced, dived down again. If he came to supper in nothing more than his swimming trunks, she would ask him to dress. She practised how she would ask. Cool would be best. Yes. She would put on the censorious tones of a Peruvian chaperon.

Would you mind putting on some clothes? I get cold just looking at you.

That sounded ridiculous! They were in the tropics, and... She thought of those intent brown eyes of his, the way they had studied *her* both clothed and almost naked.

Where I come from, we dress for dinner.

That might work if she could put a taste of amusement into the words. He might laugh. She had seen the quick light of humour in his eyes more than once. He did have a sense of humour. That was something Alan had never had. She swallowed emotion and dived deeper, pulling herself down with strong motions of her arms. She had muscles she hadn't realised, developed in those months helping at the orphanage.

If she made a joke of it, surely he would dress? If not, she could eat quickly, staring down at the fish he'd caught that afternoon. Then she would get up and leave. Yes, without even looking at him. She could thank him politely, then go upstairs. To her bedroom. To sleep.

To try to sleep. To try to forget that Max Davidson existed.

She stopped on the big patio to brush sand from her feet before she opened the screen door into the house.

'Supper's ready in ten minutes!' he called from the kitchen. 'You've just time to shower the salt away before you eat.'

'Thanks!' Had he heard her coming? She draped the towel more decorously around her shoulders, but he didn't come into the living-room. She got up the stairs and into the bedroom without seeing him. She knew it was ridiculous, but she heaved a sigh of relief when she shut the bedroom door.

She had to stop this! Millions of women could be in this position, sharing an island with a stranger, and they could *keep* him a stranger. Just because she'd had such a sheltered adolescence, because nothing had really changed in all the years of her marriage—well, that was no reason for behaving like a fool, sneaking around, afraid of her own shadow!

There was a shower in the bathroom off her bedroom. At least *that* door had a lock! She could always shut herself in here to sleep!

Lord, she was a fool!

She dressed in Cathy's jeans. The two women were the same height, although Faith had to struggle to get the zip closed. The jeans were designed for Cathy's lean legginess, not Faith's more voluptuous curves. She put a loose cotton blouse over them, and when she looked in the mirror she decided her curves were covered well enough that she wouldn't feel self-conscious even if he didn't wear a shirt. In Peru, a woman wouldn't see a man without a shirt. Not unless he was her husband and they were alone together in their bedroom. Or on the beach.

Never at the dinner-table.

When she had brushed her hair, she took out two combs from her case. Once the combs were pushed into her hair she felt better. More controlled. Her behaviour earlier seemed ludicrous. She'd been in a state of panic. The only mercy was that *he* would never know how silly she'd been.

She'd better not take any deep breaths while she was sitting across from him at the table. She didn't want her breasts to push out like that. His gaze might drop to the motion, and he'd remember the beach, where she'd stood frozen and vulnerable and—stop it!

Sandals. Yes, sandals for her feet. She had bought the sandals on that same California trip. California with Alan was a long way back. A disappointment she should have expected. She should have known by then that the marriage was nothing but a shell of pretence.

No tears. She was done with tears.

When she was halfway down the stairs, he called to her. 'Out here on the veranda!'

He had set a table up on the patio, two chairs across from each other. With the sun fading, the patio was comfortably warm. The sun set quickly in the tropics, light draining from the sky in moments. Twilight was only a brief breath of fading heat.

'You must have exceptional hearing to know I was coming down the stairs.'

She crossed to the chair he indicated. He had dressed for dinner in a short-sleeved cotton shirt and jeans. When he sat down across from her, she found herself staring at the muscular strength of his forearms.

'Comes of living alone,' he said economically.

He lived alone. If there had been a woman, she supposed he would have brought her with him. This island was made for romance, not for solitary vacations.

It was an American sort of meal. He'd prepared vegetables to go with the fish. They were tasteless, straight from a tin and cooked too long. And bread, although tortillas would have been easier to come by in this part of the world, and tastier. Only the juice beside her plate was tropical—a big glass of pineapple juice.

'It looks... thanks,' she said awkwardly. Where were her social graces gone? Why couldn't she lie and say it looked wonderful?

'The fish is good.' He shrugged. 'The rest is edible.' He grimaced at the tinned vegetables and her laugh escaped before she realised it was there.

'I get the feeling you don't normally cook your own meals.' Her voice was husky, openly curious.

He handed her the plate of fish. 'I get the feeling you don't normally cook your own meals,' he echoed, his voice teasing.

'Not when I'm in Peru.' She was glad the light was gone enough that he could not see her flush. 'But I've lived in the States as well, and in Spain.'

'Where did you learn to swim so well?'

'In Washington State when I was a child. We had a summer home on Puget Sound.' How did he know she was a good swimmer? She'd been playing in the water, alone in the world. 'You were watching me?'

'I'd no idea if you knew the basics of water safety.' He shrugged. 'You swim like a fish, and you keep inside the lagoon. You didn't need warning, so I left you to it.'

'I do know about sharks.' She tried to smile. Something in his eyes made her think wildly that he was the shark she should be wary of. She chewed on her lip, nervous and uncertain. But that look in his eyes was gone so quickly that she wondered if it had ever been there.

Had she imagined it?

She had to stop this! It was *he* who made her feel this way. Something about him, because she'd never thought so much about a man—*as a man*—since...since the summer she was nineteen.

He was talking about the island, telling her about a conversation he'd had with a local fisherman he'd met before he flew out from the Yucatán peninsula. 'You probably know all this,' he added with a dismissive wave of his hand. 'You've been here before?'

'No.' She ate another mouthful of the fish. 'I've been to Mexico, of course, but not this island.' She was hungrier than she'd thought. She hadn't eaten on the jet from San Francisco, nor the one from Mexico City to Mérida. She never ate when the earth was so far below her. Now the hunger was fierce and she reached for more of the tinned peas.

'You've never come here before? Why now? An overpowering urge to visit a tropical island?'

'An impulse.' She avoided his eyes. 'What about you?'

'Juan promised me two weeks without any possibility of seeing a woman. He was wrong.' He was grinning. Something in his eyes made it impossible for her to take offence. He didn't really mind her being here.

'Why?' she asked. 'Why didn't you want to see any women?'

He shrugged off the question and changed the subject.

She had intended to eat and run. But the last of the light faded from the sky and he seemed easier to be with. When they had finished eating, she helped him clear away. Then they sat on the shadowy patio with tall glasses of lime juice, and she told herself that she would go up soon.

Then they began to talk, lazy words with silence and night between. The moon rose and bathed them in pearl light and shadows.

They talked about the sounds, the night birds, the amazingly loud cricket that seemed to be based in that palm tree. Faith described a woman she'd seen at Mexico City airport lugging two portable computers and a three-year-old toddler. Max described his ranch in British Columbia. Shady Mountain Ranch. Broad, rolling fields of hay with a river winding through. Dark evergreen trees on the mountain behind the house. Juan's property was just around the next bend in the valley. A few miles further was the small settlement where Max's sister lived with her family. Her name was Beth and she was married to a truck logger, which made Faith yelp, 'A what?'

'A truck logger,' he repeated patiently. 'Wayne owns a logging truck, hauls timber out of the bush on contract. There's a fair amount of logging in our area.'

Beth had a three-year-old son, another baby on the way. Faith asked questions and Max answered easily enough. She formed a picture of his ranch and his sister's family, but he told her nothing about his own personal life. She guessed that he was in his late thirties, hard and confident. He lived alone, but he wasn't going to talk about that. She was good at drawing people out in conversation. She'd spent endless dinner parties in Peru pretending interest. This time the interest was real, but he didn't tell her anything private at all.

He shrugged when she asked about his parents. 'My father died a few years back. Mother's in Vancouver.' That was the end of that. Topic closed, his voice said. He was willing to talk endlessly about the ranch, his sister's family. Nothing really personal.

She began to tell him about her visit to Juan and Cathy, how Cathy had been heading for Brazil and Juan to Paris. 'They're getting together in Brazil in a few days.' She laughed and shrugged and said softly, 'It's strange to see a traditional Peruvian like Juan making room for his wife's career. They've made their base in San

Francisco because of Cathy's connection with the university there. From there, they fly off to Peru and Canada and Europe. They both seem to love it, although now the baby's coming Cathy's talking about cutting back on her travel. They've been in love since they were both very young, you know. Cathy says they made a real mess of things back then. Juan, of course, won't talk about it, although you can see how he loves her. All you have to do is watch him looking at her.'

'I have,' said Max. He pushed out of the chair he'd been lounging in. 'I'm going for a walk on the beach before I turn in.'

She was about to get up, drawn to the thought of white sand in the moonlight once the moon got free of that cloud. He made a sharp movement of protest and she understood that he didn't want her to come.

'Goodnight, then,' she said stiffly.

It was almost totally dark, but she could see his silhouette against the darker shadow of the trees. Still standing there. Staring at her, perhaps, but there was no light. What had happened? Something she'd said? She had been talking about Cathy and Juan. About how in love they were. The conversation had been lazy and easy, the words not mattering so much as the peace of the night. They must have been out here for hours. Then suddenly he had withdrawn.

The moon slipped out from behind that cloud and suddenly they were watching each other. No words, just the shock of vision where there had been only shadows.

For a second—for just a heartbeat—she thought he was going to cross the space that separated them, reach down and touch her. Something foreign pulsed in her veins. Anticipation. Excitement. Then, abruptly, he turned and she could breathe again. It was when he was a silhouette disappearing between two palm trees—then she felt relief. Then she felt the danger, when it was over.

Had anything happened at all? Could that timeless instant have been all in her imagination? If so, she should take up writing fiction. Ever since she'd landed on this island, the world had had a weird coating of unreality. Perhaps it was because she'd wanted so badly to escape her own fate for just a little longer.

Yes that was it, of course. She was making up the tension, the... the words that seemed to fill the silences between herself and this man. The make-believe helped her put off thinking about going back to Lima, where Jorge was waiting.

She went up to bed, but it was a long time before she slept. She heard him come in, heard the door downstairs and the touch of his feet coming up. She held her breath, but of course he went straight into the room next door. From the sounds she heard, he must have gone directly to bed and to sleep.

When sleep finally came to her, the dream began. A heavy fantasy of city streets. The city was Lima. There were bars at the ends of the streets. She ran down the middle of the road in her bare feet. Both sides of the streets were lined with formally dressed men. They were staring at her. Her uncles. Tio Bencho and Tio Domingo. An the end of the street she was clinging to the bars and she was the prisoner. She turned and they were all watching and Señor Jorge Sulca was walking slowly towards her, dressed in wedding finery. When she looked down, she saw that she also was dressed for the ceremony. A long white wedding dress. With a dark stain on the skirt. Below the dress her bare feet stuck out.

She struggled through the panic, woke to find herself sitting upright in the bed, panting as if she had been running, staring at the wall in front of her, slowly beginning to hear the sounds. The birds. The wind in the palms. The slow murmur of the surf.

Not Lima.

Isla Catalina.

Six more days of freedom, stolen from fate. She would not have come if she had known there was a man here, but he wasn't going to do her any harm. Last night had been... her crazy images. Sitting bolt upright in her borrowed bed, she knew she had been the one to create the discomfort. He hadn't wanted a woman around, but he'd been putting up with her pretty well. Until she started talking about Cathy and Juan. About love.

Then he had got right away from her. He had taken a lonely moonlit walk on the beach because he wasn't even interested. Any danger here was purely in her own mind. Not surprising. She was the woman who'd persuaded herself that Alan Meredith loved her all those years ago. The woman who had spent almost ten years trying to find that love in their marriage.

She had six days left. Six days, and an escort to protect her on this lonely island. Cathy had arranged the escort, and yesterday... well, the idea that Cathy had thrown her together with Max Davidson, hoping to throw her into his arms—that was ludicrous. He wasn't the sort of man to force himself on a woman, and—no matter how attractive and masculine he was—she was certainly not the sort of woman who offered herself without a wedding-ring.

Her eyes caught the gold ring on her hand. Alan's, given because he'd wanted other things from her. Not love. She jerked her hand down angrily. Hadn't she learned by now that she wasn't a woman meant for that kind of love? She was going to be practical from now on. Sensible. No flights of fancy.

The house was empty. He must be out swimming. He wasn't in the bedroom where she'd stripped off yesterday. The door was open and she could see the bed, made tidily. The sight of it sent her back to her room to make her own bed. This wasn't her sister's house in

Spain, or the Corsica mansion in Lima. No maid here. She would not forget that again. Yesterday Max had made comments that showed he expected her to be accustomed to others looking after her. She'd show him today that she knew how to fend for herself as well.

There was coffee in the pot in the kitchen. The burner under the pot had been turned off, but the coffee was still hot. She poured herself a cup, but, even with sugar and milk added, it was terrible coffee. The packet of ground coffee that she found in the cupboard was from good Mexican beans. She couldn't imagine what he'd done to it to make it taste like that.

The frying-pan in the sink must mean he'd already had breakfast. *Está bien*, but she would make lunch. She smiled as she began to rummage through the fridge. Yes, she could do much better for them than tinned peas and stale bread.

She was sitting outside on a big wicker chair with her legs curled up and a book in her lap when he came up from the beach. 'Not fishing this morning?' she asked.

He was dripping from the sea, but his hands were empty. No spear gun in his hand. Just a towel around his neck, and as he came up the stairs to the patio he used one hand and the towel to swipe at the water trickling down his forehead from an unruly lock of wet hair.

'Morning swim,' he said. 'Far as I can tell, the fish don't bite this time of morning.'

She held up the book she had started to read. It was a big novel that spanned a thousand years in the history of North America. 'Is this yours? I found it in the living-room.'

'I've finished it. Help yourself.'

'There's fresh coffee,' she told him. 'Don't worry about lunch. I'm the cook today.'

He looked sceptical, but she would show him.

She was about three pages further in the book, involved in the plight of an American Indian woman who had been taken as a slave by the neighbouring tribe, when she heard the door from the house open again. She looked up, ready for the shock of his naked chest, but he'd pulled on jeans, and a T-shirt that did nothing to conceal the muscular chest. He had a steaming mug in his hand.

'What the hell did you do to this coffee?' he demanded.

'Is something wrong with it?' Could he possibly *like* that vile brew he'd made?

He pushed one hand through his half-dry hair. Something strange happened to her heartbeat. A man had no right to look the way he did, hard and muscular and somehow so...so...

He took another big mouthful. 'It's great. How the hell did you do it?'

She laughed then, and he grinned.

When he disappeared back into the house, it was a moment before she could see the words on the page she was reading. She was suddenly intensely glad there was no way to escape the next few days.

Would he grin like that when he tasted her cooking? As if he couldn't really believe food could taste so good?

He was a man accustomed to fending for himself. He didn't worry much about what he ate. Food was food. She smiled and went back to her book. She'd teach him differently. With the basic fare of their combined food stores, and a bit of help from the sea, she would show him good food. She seldom had the chance to cook, but she loved turning a kitchen into a place filled with good smells. Her mother had been a fantastic cook. Faith had spent hours in the kitchen in her youth, watching and tasting and learning. Even when she'd been married to

Alan she'd got their maid in Lima to show her how to prepare some of the tasty Peruvian dishes.

When Max Davidson went back to his ranch in Canada, he was going to miss her cooking. She'd make sure of that. It would be fun teaching him that he shouldn't judge people by stereotypes. He'd be forced to admit that Faith Corsica was more than a sheltered member of Peru's idle rich.

CHAPTER FOUR

FAITH couldn't believe it had been four days. It seemed only hours.

No, she amended. It seemed like forever. Time simply did not exist. Not here. Sometimes she wondered if there was still a world out there, beyond the bounds of Isla Catalina and the lagoon where they swam.

Four days, and she'd seen Max's expression at mealtimes change from wariness to eager hunger. He had turned the kitchen completely over to her and she was revelling in it. When she wasn't cooking, she swam and read and wandered. It was a small island, but except for mealtimes they avoided each other during the day. He swam in the early morning while she read. She swam later in the morning. Then she would go into the kitchen and he'd be out on the patio, reading another big book. She wished she'd brought a couple of romances with her, something light to read. She was enjoying the historical novel she'd borrowed from him, but a book like that was more work than leisure. With the sun overhead and the smell of the sea all around, she was beginning to enjoy the sensation of decadent sun-worshipping.

They both stayed under cover in the afternoons out of respect for the intense sun. As the heat eased, Max usually went spear fishing, then he would clean his catch for her before she used what he called magic to turn it into a gourmet meal. Until dark fell, they didn't spend much time together, although she was aware of him always. Mercifully, the discomfort was gone, that painful awareness of him. It was crazy that she was so aware of him—some chemical thing—but at least she'd managed to keep it secret.

It was the evenings she loved. Lazy conversations out on the patio in the moonlight. It had become a ritual, something that followed the evening meal as naturally as the water caressed the sand. Max in the big easy-chair. Faith on the wicker sofa that was positioned to look out at the moonlight shining on the sea, her legs tucked up beside her. She could not remember a time when she had been as happy as she was during those shared hours.

It seemed there was an unspoken agreement between them that the conversation would not probe or discomfit. They talked of her impressions of Spain, his of Greece, where he'd gone for a holiday the year before, and of New Zealand, which neither of them had ever seen, but Max said he'd always wanted to. They talked of the Incas who had once ruled her country, of the wildness that had been his. He told her about some of the characters he'd known and, when her laughter faded, she could feel the warmth of night and his nearness. She caught herself wondering what it would be like for a woman in his arms.

Abruptly, she began to talk about her last year in Spain.

Four days, and they'd become friends, but tonight the moon was full and Faith felt strange, frightened in a way that left her breathless and uncertain of what it was she feared.

'Why did you go to Spain?' he asked abruptly. 'You were there a long time, weren't you?'

'A year and a half.'

'Why?'

She drew the palm of her hand down along the fabric of Cathy's jeans. Why had she fled to Anita's home in Spain? To forget. To find something to live for. Mostly to get away from the past. She pushed her hair back with a hand that became entangled in the curls. She pulled out one comb, caught her hair back with it again.

'You don't have to tell me,' he said quietly.

'No, I know.' She dropped her hand from her hair, curled the fingers in. 'After the accident, I needed a change.'

'The accident?'

'When Alan died.' She still couldn't really say the words, but she remembered too clearly. The little plane, the wild turbulence in the Andes as they'd tried to fly through the pass between two mountains. 'It was an accident.'

He touched her. That was when she realised that he had moved, that he was sitting beside her on the sofa. She wet her lips with her tongue. His features were clear in the moonlight. His frown made the laughter line deep, emphasising the seriousness of his expression.

'How?' he asked gently.

She could not say the words. The pictures were too clear. The mountains, so high there was snow. The small plane. Afterwards...

Max touched her hand. She saw her fingers grip his.

'I hate remembering.' Her confession came out trembling.

'I'm sorry it hurts you,' he said softly.

If she talked she might cry. 'I went to Spain after a while. I had a cousin there. Anita. Second cousin—first cousin once removed.' She shrugged, tried to smile at the confusion of translating Spanish relationships into English. She pulled at her hand, but he would not let it free. His grip was tight on her fingers, almost painful. 'Peruvian families get complicated. Anyway...' She tried to be brisk, to dismiss that moment when she'd felt the memories too close, the baby... gone. 'So I went to visit Anita. She's married to a doctor—Antoine. He's French, actually, but she met him when she was...' She made a futile gesture with her free hand.

He touched her face with gentle fingers. 'How long has it been since your husband died?'

The sounds. She remembered the sounds as if they had been yesterday. The wind, wild and cold from a high mountain storm. The man who had married her for her family—Alan with the life gone from his body. The pain. Trapped. Alone. So empty and alone. The blessed fog coming to take her into sleep... unconsciousness.

'What—what's the date?' she demanded in a shaken voice.

His thumb stroked her jaw absently. 'The twelfth.'

When she'd woken in the hospital they'd told her she'd lost her unborn child and her husband. They'd never told her whether it was a girl or a boy. She had not asked to know the sex of the baby then. Later she'd needed to know, but she'd been gone by then, hiding in Spain and trying to bury the pain with the children in the orphanage.

'Two years.' Her voice pretended to be steady. 'Two years today.'

He cursed softly, then her face was crushed against the warm dryness of his throat. She felt the wetness. From her own tears. She had not known they'd escaped.

She choked back memories, pushed her hands against his chest to find space, to stop his arms tempting her to let go of the tears. But he was still holding her, his hands on her shoulders, fingers curved as if to draw her back protectively. She managed something that might have been a laugh if the sob hadn't caught at it.

'Sorry. I don't normally...' There weren't any words for this.

'Do you want to talk about it?' He released her and there was night between them.

She could feel her own breathing, lungs filling and emptying. She shook her head. If she talked, she would do more than cry. If she cried... She'd only really cried those tears alone, could not let it happen with Max watching, seeing the parts of herself she must keep hidden.

He leaned back. She felt the distance he deliberately placed between them. She wanted that space. She was grateful that when he spoke; his question seemed casual. 'What did you do while you were in Spain? I can't really imagine you as a lady of leisure.'

'Can't you?' She decided that must be a compliment. She bent her head, slid the combs out once again to cover her confusion.

'Not after spending these last four days with you.'

'The most energetic thing I've done is worked my way through that massive tome you brought to read.'

He had that lazy smile she loved to watch playing around his lips. 'And collected a gross of sea shells, not to mention cooking some of the most delicious food I've ever tasted. Do women of your class do their own cooking in Peru? In Spain?'

'Class?' she echoed.

'From what I've seen of Juan, I doubt anyone in the Corsica family has to do their own dishes.'

'No,' she admitted. 'Although perhaps Cathy might manage to get Juan to dry a dish. It's something I could see her doing, just on general principle.'

Amused, he agreed. 'Juan's wife is definitely not any compliant Peruvian girl.'

'No, but I suppose I am. I have been, mostly.'

'Your mother was American?'

'Yes. But—well, the American part of me isn't...' She grimaced. 'That's not really the most effective part of me. My attempts at rebellion—I don't think the American part of me works very well.'

'Didn't you say you were brought up in the States?'

'Until I was fourteen. I moved to Peru after my parents died. My uncles insisted. Juan's father and Tio Bencho.' She pushed her palms against her thighs, felt restlessness sharp and uncomfortable. 'In Spain—I told you Anita's husband is a doctor?' She smiled and spread one hand in a gesture that brushed aside frowns and tears. 'He's got some family money, which is a good thing, because they're in a little village and he's paid in chickens as often as in cash. They do have a maid, although Anita's not the type to get upset about her cousin helping out. But—no, I didn't cook much at Anita's. I helped Antoine sometimes with nursing. And I did some cooking in the orphanage.'

'Is there any end to the layers?'

Her eyes widened when he took one of her hands and began to play absently with her fingers. Did he realise he was doing that? Touching her? The way a man might touch a woman he was intimate with.

'Every day,' he murmured softly, 'I peel away another layer of Faith Corsica. When I first saw you...' His hand stilled and suddenly there was tension, crackling and dangerous.

The beach. Her headlong rush towards the water. Those inadequate scraps of lace, the only covering. His eyes—and suddenly she knew it had been a caress—his gaze on the cleavage of her breasts, the slender curve of her belly above her bikini panties.

'Please don't talk about that—on the beach. I...'

'You were embarrassed. Self-conscious.' His thumb stroked the sensitive inner flesh of her palm.

'Yes.' She felt his eyes on her. Even with shadows and night she felt naked. As if she had stripped again to those brief scraps of lace. Could he hear the pounding of her heart?

'And very beautiful.'

She stared at his hand, touching hers.

'Layers,' he said huskily. 'I wanted to peel away the layers then. There wasn't much that could be taken off...'

'Please don't!'

'No,' he agreed in a husky voice. 'It's best if I don't.'

The crickets made their night sound, drowning out the faint motion of the water. It was time to pull away, to go upstairs. It was dangerous here. The sort of danger she had been sheltered from always. Danger, and she must move quickly to protect herself from the crackling threat in the air.

'Faith...I thought you were a sun-worshipper off a wealthy yacht.' His voice softened. 'When I saw how self-conscious you were, how frightened...and the wedding-ring...and I thought...' He dropped her hand. 'Your honeymoon, I thought.' She shivered at the sudden chill in his voice. 'How far back was the honeymoon, Faith?'

'Eleven years.' There hadn't really been a honeymoon. The illusion had not lasted that long.

He pushed back his hair with one hand. 'I thought you were a cruel joke of fate. I came to Isla Catalina looking for solitude. The last thing I needed was a sexy woman who was obviously terrified I'd turn into a rampaging monster.'

'I didn't think that. I——'

'Didn't you?'

She had been aware of him. Too aware. Uncomfortable with her own reaction. She drew her bottom lip between her teeth. 'I've never been in this sort of situation. Alone like this.'

'Why the hell did you come here alone? It's not the sort of thing a woman like you would do.'

She turned her face away from his gaze. 'What kind of woman am I?'

'God knows.' He sounded frustrated. 'I've been through a dozen categories for you. You don't fit any of them.'

'Do I need a category?' She pushed away an undefined feeling of danger. Just talk—nothing to fear—but her pulse was uneven and she had to work to keep her breathing silent.

The black form of a big bird flew across the face of the moon. Max turned his head to follow the black shape. 'I'd like to put you in a category. It would be easier. I—no! Forget that.' She heard him give an explosive sigh. 'Tell me about the orphanage.'

She smoothed her hand along the denim of Cathy's jeans again. The roughness made her hand tingle. It excited her that he was disturbed about her. It made her think of... forbidden things. 'I told you it's a smallish village where they live. There's an orphanage in the village, run by the nuns. I spent a lot of time there, helping. Cooking sometimes, talking with the children. Helping with the... the babies.'

'You never had children?'

She stood abruptly. 'No. We—I—I wanted...' She went to the post that held the corner of the rail. She clasped her hands around it.

He was behind her, hands on her shoulders. 'I didn't mean to say anything more to hurt.' He squeezed her shoulders lightly before he released them. 'So how did you turn up here in blue jeans? Alone, and in blue jeans. Or, at least——' he broke off with what might have been a laugh '—the first time I saw you, you weren't in jeans, were you?'

Her flesh flamed so hotly that even in moonlight he would have seen. She kept her face averted from him. 'I needed a few days alone before I went back to Lima, and Cathy...'

She remembered just in time that she had not wanted to tell him that Cathy had deliberately sent her here. She didn't want him to think she'd been thrown into his arms. She cleared her throat. 'Cathy said I should come any time.' And Juan? Max had to know Juan was too Latin to encourage any female to journey alone to a remote island.

Mercifully, he changed the subject. 'Every time I see you in those jeans, you look as though you're expecting someone to tell you that you shouldn't be wearing them. You don't strike me as a blue-jeans girl.'

'I'm not.' She should never have come here, never have succumbed to the temptation to escape. 'It's not the way I'd dress in Peru, or in Spain. It's normal in the States, but I haven't lived there very much. Only visits since I was fourteen. And—well, I guess this whole trip to Isla Catalina is just pretend. Pretending to be someone I'm not. They're Cathy's jeans. I borrowed them.' She was smoothing her hands down them again. She clenched her fingers to stop the nervous motion. 'Coming here was the kind of impulse Cathy might have given in to. I was... stealing a week from my fate.'

When she turned she could feel the strength... could smell the masculine heat in him. She wondered why he had come, why he had not wanted to see any woman here. If someone had hurt him, it did not show in his eyes. He didn't seem a man who would allow himself to need any woman beyond comfort.

'What's your fate, Faith?'

She shrugged. 'I can't drift forever. Decisions to be made.' The factory Alan had gained out of his marriage to her, now part of his estate. The pressure from her uncles to resolve her future. 'Spain was only a vacation from reality. I knew it couldn't last forever. I have to do something. I can't just... I want... I had to decide.'

'What is it you want?'

With his question so quiet on the night, she almost felt she could answer from her heart. She wanted love. The kind of love Cathy had. The kind of love Faith Corsica had never inspired in a man.

That was the dream, but she had learned to be real, to be practical. 'I thought about staying in Spain. Staying—I could have stayed there, helping at the orphanage. I could have done that forever, but—they weren't my children.'

'You want children?'

'Yes. I—I was...' She shook her head. She couldn't say it. His hands rubbed her shoulders, caressing, reassuring. 'I was pregnant,' she said on a whisper. 'When Alan died...I—we'd tried for so long...' She hadn't the courage to tell him that it wasn't Alan who had wanted the child, that she'd needed a child desperately to pretend this marriage was a family. 'I lost the baby.'

She stood in the shelter of his arms, feeling the warmth from him. 'Oh, damn,' she whispered. 'I don't want to cry. I don't know why I tell you these things.'

'Because I'm safe.' His hands soothed her back. 'You can tell me anything. After next Wednesday you'll never see me again.'

'Wednesday...' How could she feel pain, when she had only known him four days? She began speaking to cover her confusion. 'I have a flight to Mexico City, then overnight there. Then—then I'm flying to Peru the next day, and when I get there...' She took a shaky breath. 'When I get there, Jorge will want his answer.' She closed her eyes. 'Then the wedding plans begin. I suppose...I suppose it will be a big wedding.'

His hand on her back was frozen.

She tried to step back. She could feel his shock. She remembered clearly how Cathy had reacted when Faith had confided her decision.

'In Peru,' she explained defensively, 'there aren't many choices for a widow. She can be the chaperon, watching the young girls. Or she can marry again, if someone wants her. And...'

'And this man *wants* you?'

She shivered. 'You think I should join the chaperons?'

'You've no other choices?'

'In Peru——'

'Who's forcing you to go back to Peru?'

'The only family I have is there.' Suddenly his touch was a prison and she pulled away from it. She moved restlessly down the steps from the patio, out on to the sand. When she stopped prowling she was between two tall palms, staring out over the sea. She turned, looked back. His silhouette showed him motionless. Watching her? She could feel anger in his silence.

'Do you think I'm a coward, then? Because I care what my family wishes?'

'If you ask the question,' he growled, 'perhaps it's *you* who believe you lack courage.'

He was closer now, at the top of the stairs. She reached out defensively with one hand. She must seem a coward compared to a woman like Cathy, who had the courage to make her own path despite the conventions.

'Is that what you think, Faith?' Something in his voice made her shiver despite the warmth of the night. 'Are you a coward?'

She stared down at the tangle that was her own hands, fingers locked together. 'I chose for myself once a long time ago. I was young and very reckless. When I came here, I just wanted...a few days.' She turned away. He was watching her. Judging her. 'I wanted to pretend I had the kind of courage Cathy has. That I could step off the edge of my world and...' She didn't know why she was trying to explain to him. He was silent, probably wishing she'd shut up. She would. In a minute she'd go in, go upstairs and close the door to her room.

Silence. Even the crickets. 'Jorge doesn't love me,' she whispered. 'It's not as if I'm... deceiving him. It's a business thing, a family thing. There have been... negotiations. My uncles and Jorge, and it's sort of a...'

'A merger?'

They were both talking in whispers, the rail of the veranda between them.

'Yes,' she agreed. 'A merger.'

'But you'll be sharing this man's bed?'

'Yes.' She trembled.

'Only a moment ago, you were crying for your husband.'

The grief in her marriage had begun long before she lost her husband. If the tears were for Alan, they were for failure. She heard the sound of Max's feet on the patio. He moved around the edge of the rail. Down the steps. He was going to touch her again. Closer, down the second step, then the third, and when he reached her...

He was going to tell her what a fool she was. He was a gringo, a man of the north. A man accustomed to power in his own world. He would never understand how it was for a woman in *her* world. Even Cathy, married to a Latin man, had not understood that going along with her uncles' wishes was Faith's only real choice.

She was staring up at him. Her fingers lost their grip on each other. Her hands dropped to her sides. She waited, her breath piled up in her chest, her lungs aching.

'Don't you think this is a decision that could wait a while?' His voice was soft with reason. 'Considering that the anniversary of your husband's death throws you into shock, you're hardly ready to marry.'

The ocean let up a breath of night. She felt the coolness on her bare arms. She gripped her elbows with her hands, arms wrapped around herself.

'Jorge is... a business associate of my uncle's and he's—he's been over to Spain twice, to see me, to ask me.' She shrugged. 'And one of my uncles—he's been as well—and I've had letters from my other uncle and my aunt. And... there are business reasons. I promised my answer when I got back.'

'But first you had to come here?' He made a sound like a growl. 'Because you can't bear to face the man you plan to join your life to?'

'No! It's not like that.'

'Exactly how is it?' He prowled towards her so fast that she jerked back in panic.

'Max! Don't! I... this isn't—not your affair!'

'No,' he agreed grimly. 'No, it's not. Not my affair that you're planning to sell yourself. A business deal. Family business. Who the hell do you think will thank you? And why, Faith? Because you want the child you lost two years ago? Because you want your husband back?' His voice rose sharply. 'I'm no expert on marriage, but when a man wants a business merger and a woman wants a baby and a ghost—that's not a relationship.'

'Not everyone can have love wh-when they get married.'

'You're damn right they can't! But not everyone gets married to reach for a ghost.'

'No,' she whimpered. 'That's not it.' Jorge would be a good substitute for Alan. Both men cared passionately about wealth, about business. But in her country a marriage needn't be... Perhaps this marriage *was* impossible.

She could hear Max's harsh breathing, could feel his anger on the tropical night. A stranger, but he cared more than Jorge ever would. Jorge would protect her, would... *Could* she bear to share his bed? The only man in her life had been Alan. She'd loved him when they married, had loved him as well as she could when she'd discovered that he was not the man she'd believed. But Jorge—he was more like an older brother, a remote older brother, and until this moment, with Max glaring at her and the thought of a marriage bed graphic in her mind, until now, she had avoided picturing what would happen after the ceremony.

When Max's fingers brushed her arm she panicked.

'I'd better go... I... go to bed.'

'Say his name, Faith.' His hands came down on her shoulders. Not enough light, only the soft glow of moonlight, but his voice was carved in stone and his face might have been etched by a sculptor and placed under the moon.

'Whose name?' she breathed.

'The man you'll marry.'

'Jorge.' She shivered.

His hands glided on the naked flesh of her upper arms. 'Will he love you?'

'He'll be kind,' she whispered.

She told herself she was frozen, afraid. Alone like this, his hands on her. Sliding down her back. Pressing her closer. There should be a chaperon somewhere. A voice cutting the touch to nothing. She stared at his face and her heart was heavy, beating, frightened enough that he must see.

'What about later, Faith? What happens when you come alive again? When you're ready for a living man's love? Will Jorge give you what you need?'

She could feel his heat, her own flesh shivering with panic. His lips, fuller in silhouette than she remembered. 'What are you going to do?' she breathed.

'Kiss you.' Harsh voice. His mouth a line of force coming closer.

'It's not... not a good idea.'

'You're right.' His mouth was so close that she could feel the words he spoke. 'It's a rotten idea. The worst mistake I've made in months, but—I'm going to kiss you anyway.'

The time for running was gone. Perhaps there had never been a time to run from this. Max's lips almost touching hers, the warmth of his breath on her face. Her back burned with sensation as his hands moved over the fabric of her blouse. His mouth settled on hers. Warm. Soft.

The trembling started as his mouth brushed across her lips. He took her lower lip in his possession, then the corner of her mouth. His hands tightened on her back and suddenly everything changed and there was nothing anywhere but his touch.

Mouths clinging, hers to his, and his tongue finding the softness and the entry to the dark shadows. Taking. Deeper, spinning, his embrace hardening, and she was pressed against his need, head tilted back into the cradle of his arm. Her world was spinning with his mouth taking, and when his tongue asked she offered and there was only the growing heat.

Fire flowing, a river of flame in the moonlight. Flames that seared her woman's flesh and brought a cry from her throat, high and formless. His kiss spread to her throat and his body shifted. His hunger, her flesh answering.

He lifted his head. Silence. Heartbeats pulsing.

Her eyelids were heavy, swollen from his touch. She dragged them open. His hands slid down her body and cupped her buttocks. She moaned, her body pressed intimately to his. Passion flashed in his face, heat in the shadows and his gaze on her. She felt the sound that escaped her throat, and this was what they meant in the books. This was need and hunger and passion, and a woman must reach for fulfilment or she would die from the pulsing flame that flared higher and higher and out of...

He released her so suddenly that she cried out, unable to hold back the protest. For a disjointed second, she thought she would sink to the sand underfoot without his arms to hold her.

'Go to bed.'

Her eyes struggled to focus on the long, hard form of the man only inches away. The shiver crawled down her back. If she reached out, she could touch him. A second ago... warmth, heat consuming her.

'For God's sake, Faith—get out of here while you can.'

'Please...' A whisper of sound. Her sound. She did not know what the plea meant, knew only that turning to leave would tear something new and fragile inside her. She flushed, felt the heat, and if he saw it made no difference in that instant.

'Go! What do you imagine I'm made of?'

She sucked in a torn breath. 'I—I didn't——'

'Get out of here.' Harsh voice. Angry words.

He'd kissed her. *She* was the one who had gone up in flames. He sounded tired, perhaps bored with her. She turned away, her steps uneven on the stairs up to the patio, her hand pressed to her mouth. Would his kiss burn there forever?

'Goodnight, Faith.'

She turned back. 'Why did you do that?' she asked, her voice trembling. Her entire body felt swollen. Only a moment in his arms, but she might never be the same again.

No answer.

She opened the screen door and went into the beach house. Up the stairs. Down the short corridor to her bedroom. The room next to his. No connecting door. More than a kiss. Flames. Consuming her. Like a brand on her, except that he was back there, on the sand, and he had watched her go when he must have known she needed to stay.

There was nothing he wanted from her.

She heard him come up the stairs. She was still dressed, staring at the door. His sounds told her that he had gone into the other bedroom. Her hand was on her blouse, but she could not make herself unfasten it until she heard him leave again, until the screen door slammed downstairs and he was gone.

She was alone in the house.

She unfastened her blouse, then the metal button at the waist of Cathy's jeans. When her clothes were gone, she jerked the soft luxury of her nightgown over her head and dived under the covers. In the moonlit shadows of her bedroom, she stopped trying to tell herself that she should have done something to stop him. There was nothing she could have done.

She had no idea how it had happened. She certainly didn't know why. Somehow Max had caught possession of her heart. It was crazy to believe that she could be in love with a man she'd only known for four days, but...

No! Surely not love. Not in four days!

She'd read the books. This was infatuation. Four days, and it could only be...physical...lust. She hadn't realised lust could happen to her, had not dreamed that she could be in a man's arms, his touch and his mouth on hers the world. Nothing anywhere but sensations and the man and the passion.

It had not been like that for him. When he'd kissed her he had been angry, his northern personality shocked at the Latin arrangement of her coming marriage. He'd been trying to prove her wrong, trying to destroy the inevitability of her Latin fate with one angry kiss. It was a Canadian man's way of protesting, of showing his outrage at her lack of emancipation.

He couldn't know what had happened to her. If he had not pulled back, nothing could have enabled her to break away from him. When he touched her, it was as if... as if his heart owned hers.

No! Not hearts! It was the moon.

Chemistry. Yes, chemistry. It had gone to her head, because she had so little experience and she hadn't expected it. She'd been a virgin when she married. There had never been anyone but her husband. She'd never dreamed the temptation of sex could be strong enough to erode her vow to have intimacy only within the bonds of marriage.

If Max Davidson touched her again... if he kissed her and asked for more...

CHAPTER FIVE

FAITH made pastries in the kitchen, little pastries she had watched the maid in Anita's home make. They were fussy and complex and Faith needed that, her eyes on the mixture of flour and water and spices.

Cathy and Juan had left a well equipped kitchen. Faith found supplies secured in safe metal containers, preserved from moisture and insects. It was not Faith's flour, not her spices, but she had to have something to occupy her hands, something to focus on.

Max was out somewhere. It was a small island, but this was their second day with no more than polite words. Yesterday—the day after that explosive kiss—the atmosphere of Isla Catalina had been crackling with tension. No words, no more than necessary. 'Supper is ready,' she'd said. Then, 'Goodnight, I'm going up.' He'd nodded and muttered and she wasn't meant to hear the words, nor to answer or ask questions.

When she'd said goodnight, he had not looked up from the book he was reading. No shared hours on the patio last night. He'd read all evening and she'd gone out to walk on the beach, away from him. All the time avoiding talk—knowing he was avoiding her as well. All that time she had felt the dullness inside, her future pressing against her consciousness.

One more day. Then home to Peru. To her family.

To Jorge.

She would never see Max again.

She knew she was in no state to make a decision. She had hardly slept the night Max kissed her. She had been awake when the moon had set and his footsteps had finally come softly up the stairs. Then silence, and he must have slept, but it was hours before she had. Staring at the dark ceiling, blind, not knowing what he was thinking...what he was feeling. Then, last night, the dreams had been worse than the waking, and now she was trying to drive the unease away with her hands in the pastry dough.

Max Davidson had tumbled her world upside-down.

He was outside, lying in a hammock slung between two big palm trees, reading a book. Yesterday, in desperation, she had tried to read. The words had been nonsense, and reading when her life was in chaos was insane!

What was she going to *do*?

Two nights ago...words in the moonlight...touching. A kiss that had destroyed everything she had believed about herself. How long would that kiss take to fade? She tried to remember Alan's touch, his lips on hers. He'd been her *husband* and she could not remember! She reached back into yesterday, but there was nothing but a memory of disillusionment. No sensations, just memories.

Old memories. That heady summer when she was nineteen and in love. She had dreamed then, images of fantasy. She had believed that her blood would flame, that she could be like the heroine of one of the romances her aunt loved to read.

The reality of marriage had taught her that a woman learned to accept what she had: the companionship of other women; children, if God meant there to be children; a husband who protected and sheltered and slew dragons, keeping the world from threatening his wife.

Passion...some women had passion, but Faith had no choice but to accept that a passionate love was not meant for the woman who had been born Faith Corsica.

She remained a Corsica. In Peru a woman kept her birth name after marriage. Her husband ruled her, but she retained her name.

She'd learned not to be a dreamer. She had accepted reality and made the best of it. No point in struggling against what life handed her. Love was for the novels and lucky people like Cathy and Juan.

Until Max had touched her, and two days later she was still in shock. Just a kiss, and he might laugh if he knew, but those moments in his arms—it could be an obsession if she let it take over. She punched her fist into the pastry. She *refused* to spend her life yearning for a crazy moment under the palms! She'd better find her balance, and fast!

She turned to look out of the kitchen window. Max's hammock was motionless under the palms. Did he regret those moments in the moonlight as much as she did? She *had to* regret them! There was no other choice for her. This was Tuesday. Tomorrow her helicopter would come.

Jorge...

She pushed her palm into the mixture that would become succulent pastries if her emotions did not contaminate the baking. She closed her eyes and she could feel her hands helpless, caught under Jorge's touch.

He was a good man. Steady and sincere. He would be an honourable husband. Not completely faithful, perhaps. Many men in her culture kept a mistress. Alan had, despite the fact that he was an American. It was considered acceptable in Peru, so long as the relationship was discreet.

Jorge would be... discreet.

She opened her eyes. Her hands were all flour and shortening. She felt as if she had been cut loose, as if she were floating, with nowhere to rest, no place that was hers. Marriage to Jorge... his touch on her flesh.

Impossible now. She would shudder when he touched her. She would remember Max's hands sliding down the curve of her back, would remember how her body had pressed against Max. Needing him.

Worse than physical adultery... marrying one man while another burned in her body.

The helicopter would come tomorrow and she would never see Max again. He would stay on the island for three more days until the seaplane he'd chartered came for him. Then he would fly back to Canada, to his ranch. With luck, he would never realise he had turned her life upside-down. She had never *needed* before. Not like that.

She would go back to Peru, but marriage was impossible now. She wasn't sure she had the courage to face all that displeasure. Her uncles could be intimidating. It would be difficult, telling them she would not marry Jorge. Tio Bencho would remind her that she'd virtually promised when he'd visited her in Spain last month. Faith had promised an answer on her return to Lima and they'd both known it would be yes. Anita had shrugged afterwards and said Jorge was a good man.

He was. But...

If only Max had never touched her! If he had been trying to persuade her that she couldn't marry Jorge, he'd succeeded far better than he knew. If she'd never woken to the flames that were lying sleeping inside her...

What *was* she going to do?

She put the pastries in the oven. With the sun heating her world, she had to get out of the kitchen with its radiating oven. She was hot, baking in Cathy's jeans.

She was going for a swim.

Upstairs, she changed into her swimsuit and threw a big towel around her shoulders. She passed Max on her way down to the beach and for a second they both seemed frozen, the sun beating down on them. Staring. Eyes caught. Her legs naked, the towel draped around her neck to cover her upper body. Max in bathing-trunks and a cotton shirt unbuttoned to the waist.

'I'm going swimming,' she muttered. Dressed in a bathing-suit, heading for the water! Of course she was going swimming!

He nodded abruptly.

'I'll be back before the pastry is ready to come out of the oven.' He certainly wasn't interested. She pressed her lips together and rushed on towards the water, knowing he was watching her. She pulled the towel more tightly around her, wishing it would cover her legs.

Then she dropped the towel on the big rock at the water's edge, and something made her turn to face him.

He was gone.

The pastries were burned.

Faith took the baking-sheet out of the oven, cursing softly so that the words were indistinct. She dropped the tray on to the ceramic counter. Behind her, she heard the sound of bare feet on the floor tiles. Max.

'They're burned,' she muttered. She swung around belligerently. She wanted to tell him to go away. It was ridiculous, but she might cry, and his opinion of her was low enough already. She didn't want to add crying over a stupid bunch of pastries.

She jumped back when he reached past her to pick up the tray. 'Go outside,' he commanded. 'Under the trees where it's cool. I'll look after this.'

'I'll...'

'I'm sorry.'

'It's just a dozen pastries.' She blinked away the tears. 'It doesn't ma-matter.' Her voice warbled on the last word.

Mercifully, he ignored the fact that she was on the verge of tears. He had the cover off the bin and was efficiently dispatching the contents of the baking-tray into the bin. She skirted around him to turn off the oven.

'I'm sorry about the other night,' he said. 'That's what I meant.'

'Oh.' The beach. His kiss. She smoothed her hand down the front of her bathing-suit. It was so hot outside. Hotter in here. 'I—it—doesn't matter.'

'Doesn't it?' He stood erect.

'No.' She would dream of him forever.

'I think it does. It isn't like you to burn things.'

Her head lifted. 'You don't know me.' Her words were quietly aggressive. 'You don't know what sort of woman I am.'

'I know you haven't talked to me in the last two days.'

'You didn't want talk. You came here to be alone.'

'Faith...'

'I'm going outside.'

'Not yet.' His hand flashed out to imprison her wrist.

'You—let go of me.' Her words seemed dull, without conviction. She could feel her pulse racing under his fingers. She had to tilt her head back to look at his face. He was so close, so much taller than she was. His eyes were narrowed, studying her face. Seeing what?

His mouth turned down, the frown echoed in his eyes. 'There's not much sense my trying to explain why I kissed you.'

'No,' she agreed. 'Let go of me.'

'I had no right.'

'No, you didn't.' She had not exactly fought him off.

'It's none of my business who you decide to marry.' His fingers tightened their grip on her wrist. His eyes flared with memory and she gulped.

'Let me go. Please, Max.'

He stared at her imprisoned hand for a long moment. 'The hammock's free,' he said quietly. 'Why don't you take a book and relax in the shade?'

'I've lunch to cook.'

'Go on,' he urged. He freed her hand. 'It's my turn to be cook.'

'I can't just sit around while you——'

'Can't you?'

She found she could smile, an answer to the curve that had appeared on his lips. He turned her and gave her a gentle shove in the direction of the kitchen door.

'Go!'

She went.

He brought tortillas and cheese, a simple meal outside under the palms. He pulled up a small table near the hammock, and brought a beach chair for himself. Then he wrapped a tortilla around a piece of cheese and handed it to her. She shifted herself in the hammock, trying to sit up.

'Don't bother. Relax and eat.'

'In the hammock?'

'Pretend you're a Canadian,' he suggested with a smile in his voice. 'You don't need place-settings and a dining-table to have lunch when you're out of doors.'

She took a bite of the tortilla, gave up trying to get into a more dignified position. It was impossible in a hammock! 'In Peru, even when we have back-yard barbecues, it's fairly formal. The women wear dresses and make-up, and there are plates and—ordered seating.'

He rolled another piece of cheese into a tortilla for himself. 'Bad for you, all that formality.'

It was nice, lying back in the hammock nibbling on tortillas. He gave her another when she finished the first. She pushed back the uneasy sense of guilt that came from all those years being chaperoned. If she turned her head, she could watch him, but even that seemed an effort. When she'd finished the glass of lime and water he gave her, she sank back and let her gaze explore the palm leaves overhead with idle enjoyment.

She could feel him close by. He was in no hurry to leave her. A moment like this could be forever. The awkwardness of the last two days seemed remote and unreal.

'Max?'

'Hmm?' His voice was lazy, as if he too was caught in her mood.

'Have you ever been married?' She twisted to see him as she asked the question. He was sprawled in the chair, staring up at the bit of sky visible through the palms.

'I had a close call a while back.'

He spoke as if it were an accident he'd averted. She tried to smile at the image. 'Did—did you love her?'

'I don't think I believe in love.'

'What about Cathy and Juan?'

He smiled ruefully. 'I guess—they've certainly got something. And my sister Beth has, with her husband. But for most people...' He shrugged that away and reached for another tortilla.

Faith tangled her fingers through the holes in the weave of the hammock. 'You said I shouldn't marry Jorge because... If you didn't love her, why were you going to marry her?'

'Come on, Faith!' His laughter mocked her question. 'I shouldn't have to tell you there are other reasons for getting married than eternal love.'

'What was *your* reason?'

'It seemed like time.' He stood up abruptly.

Staring up at him, she felt intense awareness of her own body lying caught in the hammock. 'Time?' she breathed.

'Yes. Time.' He made a motion as if he would push his hands into his pockets, then spread them in a half-angry gesture. 'There are seasons for everything. Last year seemed to be the season for—hell! What does it matter?'

'The season for what?'

'Marriage. Children. Family.' He snapped the words out. He shifted his shoulders and finally looked down at her. 'I'd spent fifteen years establishing the ranch. The hard part's finished now. It seemed time to—I was wrong. It was a mistake.'

'Who was she?' Faith's mouth was dry. What sort of woman would he reach for? Two days ago, under the moon, he had reached for her.

'What does it matter who she was?'

She struggled up in the hammock until she was sitting, her legs hanging over the edge. 'You asked me about Jorge. Can't I ask?'

He shrugged assent. 'She was just someone I knew. She lives in a town a few miles away, and we've been...seeing each other.'

They had been lovers. 'Does she have a name?'

'Alice.'

She would be blonde and very much a gringo. Very different from Faith with her dark Latin heritage. She pushed back the tangle of her hair. She must have left her combs on the dresser upstairs. Max and Alice. Alice in Wonderland. But his Alice would not be an innocent child. She would be... They would have done far more than exchange a heated kiss. By Max's standards, what had happened between himself and Faith on the beach the other night must seem tame.

'What...what happened? Why didn't you marry her?'

'She didn't live up to the terms of our bargain,' he said grimly.

The harshness in his voice must mean that he still cared.

She wished she had not asked the name. All afternoon it echoed in her mind. Alice. Images of a sultry blonde woman. Or perhaps she was lithe and seductive. Either way, she would be all woman, because Max would want a very feminine woman.

This was stupid! She was leaving tomorrow. One more night, then she had to get on the helicopter. She hadn't made any plans, had no idea what she would do after she landed in Mérida. Take the plane to Mexico City, then...

She had to go back to Peru. What else could she do? Alan had owned a house in Seattle, where they'd occasionally stayed, but that had been sold when the estate was wound up. She supposed there was money, enough that she didn't exactly have to worry about starving. The money and property was all in the hands of Tio Bencho, and he was probably the person who would give her the hardest time when he learned she was not going to marry Jorge. Jorge himself wouldn't be broken-hearted. Annoyed, perhaps.

The uncles would be furious.

She swam again, briefly, because the sun was growing more intense with afternoon. Then she went into the kitchen and started playing around with a recipe for supper. Maybe she'd get an inspiration about her future tomorrow.

If only it were Max waiting for her in Peru instead of Jorge. She trembled as she thought of his touch.

Having fantasies about a stranger she'd never see again had to be worse than insane! She and Max were worlds apart. But at least they were talking again. She'd missed his company so much during those endless hours of tension. She flipped open the recipe book she'd found in a drawer and decided that if there were only a few hours left she would make the most of them.

'My farewell party,' she announced when she brought their supper to the table that evening. He'd been swimming, had brought back fish for their breakfast tomorrow. She had laid the table while he was cleaning the fish. Then he'd gone to wash, and she'd lit candles and brought out the food.

When he came back down he surveyed the laden table with obvious anticipation. 'How do you do it? I go into that kitchen looking for food, and it seems there's nothing.' They shared a smile, then he said suddenly, 'Hold on! I know where there's a bottle of wine, if we're celebrating.'

He came back with wine and glasses, poured her a glass before he sat down. 'There you are! Nectar of the gods.'

It was fun. The sort of warm companionship they'd had before that kiss, made special by the bubbly excitement of the wine. Faith refused to think about tomorrow, about leaving, making decisions. She could decide as well on the mainland as here. Perhaps better, because Max would be in her past then.

She might be alone forever, but at least Max had done her the favour of showing her that marrying Jorge wasn't the answer, any more than marrying Alan had been the answer.

Max carried the wine out to the patio after they had eaten. Faith hung back, bothered by the confusion of dishes on the table.

'Leave it all,' he said, jerking his head towards the outside. 'If this is your farewell party, you're not doing dishes in the middle.'

She laughed and followed him outside. She leaned back against the screen door when she closed it, shutting them outside together. The candlelight from inside glowed gently in the window behind her. 'I've never had a party like this.'

He was filling her glass, looking up with a question in his lifted brows.

She stared at the bubbly stuff he was pouring into her glass. She was already light-headed. She moved towards the table, reached out and took the glass when he held it out for her. Their fingers brushed and she breathed in the scent of the man along with the evening sea. She lifted the glass to her lips.

'What kind of parties have you had?'

'Formal.' Her lips twitched. 'When I turned fifteen...a girl's fifteenth birthday is a very special occasion in Peru.' They were standing half a metre apart. She curled her fingers around the stem of the wine glass and buried the restlessness of her other hand in the folds of her skirt. She was wearing a gauzy blue skirt with a matching peasant blouse. She had bought it in San Francisco, although ironically it looked more Latin than anything else she had worn since coming to this island.

'And your wedding,' he asked, his eyes on hers. 'Was that a very special occasion?'

'No, we... I met Alan in the States the summer I was nineteen. We eloped.' She had to look away from him. She shook her head in confusion. They had been talking about parties. Her voice was husky. Confused. She was having trouble getting words out. 'Then we flew to Peru and...'

'So everything was fine once the family met him?'

She blinked at the sharpness in his voice. 'Yes, they accepted him.' Alan had charmed them all, her uncles and her aunts. It was only later that she understood it was what he'd planned all along. Later, when he resisted her suggestion that they return to the States. Why should he go back, when he had what he wanted here in Lima? With the aid of the Corsica family, he could easily establish his factory on the outskirts of Lima.

Tio Bencho had helped with the financing. Tio Domingo had made available a tract of land in an advantageous location. Faith had contributed her illusions. She clenched her hand in her skirt, crushing the thin fabric. What were illusions for but to give up?

'Your Alan was American?'

'Yes.' Why must he ask about Alan? He didn't like it when she probed about his past with Alice.

'But you didn't live in the States?'

She shook her head, wanting to move, to give in to the restlessness. 'Alan had... business interests in Peru. We went to the States sometimes, to the Seattle area. Not often.' Mostly Alan had made those trips alone, pushing aside Faith's suggestion that she accompany him. It was only later that she'd learned he'd had a mistress in Seattle.

'When will you stop grieving for him?'

She stared at the place on Max's chest where his third button was fastened. The button was half undone, almost escaping its hole. She touched it, frowning in concentration as she refastened it.

'Faith...'

She looked up at his face, her hand still resting on his chest. She could feel the hammer of his heart. He was staring down at her.

'Faith, you'd better... better go up... to bed.'

She drew in a shaky breath.

'Don't,' he breathed. 'Get out of here while you can.'

She could feel the heat under her hand. His heat. His heart beating. His eyes on her. 'You've had too much wine,' he said. His voice seemed fuzzy.

'Yes,' she agreed. She knew he was right. A woman could not stand with her hand resting intimately on the chest of a man who was not her husband. Her hand on him, eyes breathless, the night silent all around. A woman... a woman of breeding would never allow this to happen. And if it did, she would retreat. Fast.

'Faith.' He cleared his throat. 'Go now. If you don't...'

'What will happen if I don't go?'

She felt his chest expand with a breath of anger. No, not anger, because the air was filled with something else, something tangled and breathless.

'If you don't leave now, I'll kiss you again.'

Her fingers spread out and she could feel the roughness that was his chest hair through the shirt. She stared at the shadow of her hand, the finger still moving slightly over the hard curves of his muscles. Then she looked up into his face with only the moon to guide her gaze.

'Damn you,' he whispered. He was glaring at her, the lines around his mouth deep. His hand was at her back, pulling her against him. Not gently.

She was caught against him, mesmerised. His eyes. His mouth, lips parted slightly although he was still frowning. His body, hard against her, the swirl of her skirt settling around them as his thighs pressed into hers.

'Now will you go?' he groaned.

Her heart was hammering. He had to feel it, or perhaps it was *his* heart. His eyes, telling what his body had already revealed. Then he stepped back, releasing her so that she staggered, and she knew that it was far more than infatuation, more than lust.

She loved him.

'Aren't you going?'

'No.' Her fingers curled into her palms, but there was no warmth left.

He crammed his hands into the pockets of his jeans. 'This is no place for a virtuous woman, Faith. You've got to know that I want to take you to bed. Or take you here on the sand. Maybe it's your husband's memory that makes you soft and... that makes you feel willing in my arms, but—but if you don't get out of here now...' The harshness deepened. 'If you don't go, I'm going to stop being a gentleman.'

She swallowed three times before she could speak, before she could put words to the outrageous idea that had come to her.

'If you want me...' She sucked in a breath. There was nothing in his face to help her. She wasn't a courageous girl, but what did she have to lose? Tomorrow she would be gone. She gulped and said the words.

'You—well, you could marry me.'

CHAPTER SIX

'YOU'RE crazy!' Max's voice was shocked, too loud on the soft night.

She lifted her head. If it were light, she would be meeting his eyes with determination in hers. She wanted to run, to jerk back the words, but they were said, and it was too late for the knowledge that her offer could only be rejected.

'Woman, you've got to be out of your mind! Why in God's name should we get married?'

Because she would never see him again. Because they lived in different worlds and they'd only been together one week but she would miss him terribly when she left.

'That's no kind of joke to lay on a man, Faith!'

'I'm not joking.' She must not tell him the truth—that she was meant to be *his*. He did not believe in love for himself, and he would not listen to any claim she might make to love him. Too soon. Of course it was too soon.

'I thought it made sense,' she said in a husky voice. What could she offer him? A business deal. He would understand that, wouldn't he? He'd talked about it almost like that. The ranch in good shape, time for a wife and family. 'You wanted a family,' she reminded him. 'A wife.' She shrugged and the tears tried to come up, but she would not let them. 'I'm available, and...and...'

He turned away from her. 'I live on a ranch,' he muttered. 'In the middle of nowhere. You'd be buried out there. You...' He made an explosive sound, then a soft curse. 'You can't offer to marry every man who kisses you. You... For God's sake, Faith!'

'Not every man. You.' Her heart was hammering. 'I'm a good cook. You know that. And I don't care about the isolation.'

'Easy words to say.'

'I've spent time on the Corsica hacienda in Peru. It's in the mountains, miles from everything but a campesino village.' She sounded plaintive, begging. She had to stop. Words would not change his mind. He didn't want her. He'd wanted her body, but not at the price she'd named. She whispered. 'I'd be a good wife to you. And I'm—I'm good with babies. Children. I've...'

Oh, lord! Not tears. Not here! Please not here!

'Look, Faith...' She could hear the distaste in his voice. 'There's a sexual thing between us, but that's all. My God! You can't marry a man just because... Nothing happened!' He rammed his hands into his pockets. 'Nothing's going to happen. You can't have led that sheltered a life. One hot kiss isn't enough to marry for.'

Thank goodness he could not see her well enough to know how she was trembling. 'It's a business deal,' she insisted desperately. 'I thought you understood that.' Her breath was burning in her chest. She managed to get words past. 'I want a child, so I need a husband. And you—and you wanted a wife. You know I can cook, and I can promise I'll fulfil the rest of your... of your...'

'My needs? My physical needs?'

She gulped. 'Yes,' she whispered.

'Do I get a sample of the goods?'

She heard the faint squeak of protest from her own throat. 'If... if you want.'

'Too high a price, Faith?'

He was staring at her hands. She looked down and saw her fingers, white in moonbeams. Clenching and unclenching. She made her hands close into fists and be still. When he spoke, she looked up, but he was only a silhouette in the midst of tall palms. The moon was gone. It was dark, like his voice.

'Did you plan to make this offer tonight?'

'I...'

'Were you planning to pretend I was Alan as you made the ultimate sacrifice?' His voice hardened into anger. 'Were you going to close your eyes and see his face as I took your body?'

She gasped a wordless protest.

'I'm not about to help you keep Alan's memory alive by agreeing to this insane proposition.' His voice grew louder. 'If you're dreading what's ahead of you in Peru—well, I'm not the answer, Faith.'

Yes, he was.

'Go sleep off the wine, for God's sake!'

Morning came suddenly, the dawn flooding the sky from black to grey to blue in the space of a quarter of an hour.

Wednesday, and somehow she had to get from now to the helicopter. Past Max, who had been disgusted by her offer last night. Faith shivered, hugging herself under the blankets. She had to get up, had to pack her things and somehow get through the time until the helicopter came. How many hours until she escaped this place? Last week, asking the pilot to come back next Wednesday, it hadn't mattered exactly when. Morning, they'd agreed, because she had a plane to catch in Mérida.

She slipped out of bed and padded to the dresser in bare feet. She slid the top drawer open and took out the silver watch she'd shed on that first day. What need to think of time in this place?

Six-thirty. Sunrise at six-thirty. She strapped the watch on her wrist. Here in Mexico winter was over. In Peru, summer would be complete and the season moving into winter. What would it be like in Canada where Max lived? She could ask Juan one day, because her cousin owned a ranch that bordered on Max's.

What if she asked Juan to invite her to the ranch in British Columbia? Cathy and Juan didn't spend a lot of time up in Canada, but when they were there perhaps Faith could come, and Max would be near by on the next property.

She would not ask. She had learned that much at least—not to hang on to dreams when the reality had destroyed them. Perhaps this wasn't even a dream. The madness of one moment, his hands on her, and her whole being recognising him as her fate.

Once she had thought Alan was her fate. Her love forever. She'd been wrong that time too. That was why she'd let the uncles talk her into marriage to Jorge. Because, after Alan, a cool marriage made sense. Cool on both sides, and the uncles probably had better judgement than she did. It was prudent to trust the counsel of her elders instead of her own impulsive heart.

After ten years with Alan, she would have thought impulse was dead in her.

She changed into her swimsuit, careful to take the big towelling robe she'd found along to the beach. Only hours to get through now. There would be no accidental encounters on the beach with too much skin showing and her heart beating above the sound of the water on the rocks.

This morning the water was cold, and she gasped as she walked in. She kept moving, walking slowly until she was waist-deep. Then she closed her eyes, dived forward and struck out away from the island.

She swam until she felt the pulse of energy return to her. She had been in panic when she woke, but the cool water soothed and calmed. Of course she would be able to face Max this morning. She had years of practice at putting on a social mask. How many dinner parties in Lima, knowing it was a lie, Alan at her side acting the loving husband? A well paid role for him, because Alan had got his factory and her family's loyalty. For her...she did her duty to her husband. How many mornings, facing Alan across the breakfast-table, her face neutral and her voice quiet with politeness? A good wife did not make a scene about the destruction of her marriage, and Faith had been a good wife. She put her face down and crawled through the water with renewed energy. A few hours was nothing! She'd just——

She floundered in the water, gasping.

A hand around her waist!

She turned to his touch, spluttering water. He pulled her closer, his arm hard around her back. Max, floating in front of her, wet, naked legs tangling with hers as he trod water for both of them. Then he released her, so quickly that she must have imagined the urgency in his brief grasp.

'What are you doing?' The weight of her wet hair obscured her vision. She pushed the hair back from her face, treading water with her legs and one hand. He was a couple of feet away from her, treading water too, his eyebrows lowered, hiding any expression in his brown eyes.

'You're not planning to swim outside the reef?' he demanded. She realised that he had placed himself between her and the reef that was only yards away.

'Of course not.' She pushed at her hair again as it fell into her eyes. He must think she was a real idiot if he believed she could go swimming out there. 'I'm not about to sacrifice myself to the sharks,' she muttered. Only two days ago they'd watched the fin of a shark cruising past the island outside the reef. Faith knew shark attacks on humans weren't common—but they weren't unknown either.

'You were ready to sacrifice yourself to me last night.'

'That was a business proposition,' she retorted, turning away in the water to hide the heat she could feel rising. She took a deep breath and dived down, swimming underwater, away from him, away from the reef. When she surfaced, she looked back and saw she had left him far behind.

He'd come out to stop her going out to play with the sharks. It had not been anything personal, just that he was a man who took responsibility for others. He was accustomed to looking after the people he felt were in his charge. Perhaps because of his friendship with her cousin Juan, he felt some responsibility for Faith.

She turned and began to swim hard, heading for shore.

He was still swimming in the lagoon when she finished cooking breakfast. She ate alone, then she left his plate on the table and washed up her own. Tomorrow he would be cooking for himself. She went upstairs to shower, then changed into stockings and the silk suit.

She packed everything except the toiletries bag that would fit in her handbag. There was hardly anything left of the box of food she had brought. She would leave whatever there was behind here. Leaving, she would carry only her bag and her handbag.

She would tell her uncles she'd decided not to marry Jorge, and she'd tell Jorge as well. They'd be angry, but in time it would fade. The days when a woman was forced into marriage were gone. There was pressure these days, yes, but not force. This morning the future seemed plain and simple and bleak. Nothing. There was nothing ahead for her.

What did it matter if the uncles did not like her decision? After she told them . . . she would go away again. Perhaps she would go back to the orphanage in Spain.

In her stockinged feet, she carried the bag downstairs. She did not see Max. He must still be out swimming. She felt a tug of panic, but of course he would not be so foolish as to go outside the reef. It was stupid to worry, because he was a man who'd been looking after himself a long time. She went back up the stairs for a final check of the bedroom where she had slept so poorly these last few days. No wonder she'd been restless, with Max next door every night, her ears straining for the sound of him. She'd never before felt this crazy compulsion, this physical need for a man's touch.

It would fade. Given time, every sort of dreaming faded. Except the pain of losing her baby. That was a strong yearning that took over every time she saw a child, especially an infant. Faith sat at the vanity unit with her hairbrush in her hand, brushing hard and steadily, through the tangles the wind had made. When she had her hair tamed, she pushed the two combs in, one on either side. Alan's gift to her. The only thing he'd given her that had not been disappointment and disillusionment.

She put the brush in her handbag, pulled out lipstick and eyeshadow. When she was made up she thought she looked more confident. She stood up and slipped into her pumps. When she looked at herself in the mirror, it was the woman she knew, the woman from all those endless parties in Lima during the long years of her marriage. Smooth. Friendly yet cool. Shielded.

She walked down the stairs.

He was standing at the bottom.

'When's your chopper coming?'

'My what?' She continued down three more steps, then stopped. If he didn't move back from the stairs, she would not have the courage to go right to the bottom.

'Your helicopter. When's it coming?'

Chopper... helicopter. Of course. 'Some time this morning.' As she said the words, she thought she heard the faint echo of rotors beating the air.

He gripped the knob at the bottom of the banister with one hand. She was three steps above him.

'What are you going to do, Faith?'

She had not been sure if her formal persona would withstand coming up against his probing gaze. But for the moment, her calm held. She shifted her shoulders in a lazy Latin gesture. 'What am I going to do?' she echoed. 'I'm going to fly to Mérida by helicopter.'

A muscle jerked in his jaw. 'You know damned well that's not what I meant.'

On the third step, she was slightly above him. She met his eyes and her voice came out cool and indifferent. 'Why should I know anything of the sort?' She saw the muscle jerk in his arm, as if he'd gripped the banister hard.

'Are you going back to Peru?'

'It's my home.' She held his gaze. 'Would you move aside, Max?'

'Are you going to marry that guy?'

'Jorge?' The helicopter was closer, the sound definite. It was circling the island, choosing the spot for a landing. 'It's not any of your business who I marry.'

'Dammit, Faith!' For a moment she thought she had gone too far, that he would come up those three stairs and throttle her.

To cover her nervousness, she shifted the strap of her handbag up on to her shoulder. 'That's my helicopter landing.'

'You can't marry him.'

She took a step down, closer to him. He didn't move. She stared past him, concentrating on the place just beyond the barrier of his body. She sucked in a breath that he must have heard, but she kept her voice hard and empty. 'If you want rights over my decisions, you'll have to marry me to get them.'

It was the only thing she could think of to say, and her words made him step back. She walked past him then, not meeting his eyes, just walking. Her bag was at the door. She walked to it and bent down and she knew that for the rest of her life she would remember this. Walking away from him. His silence telling her that he would run a long way to escape marriage to Faith Corsica.

All he'd ever wanted was her body. He had a right to laugh himself silly over her proposal of marriage. She curled her fingers around the handle of her bag and shifted her balance, then pushed the screen door open. Of course he was letting her go. Why would he stop her? He'd had the urge to bed her as part of his holiday escape, but not to marry her. He was probably in love with Alice. He might go back home and repair whatever damage had been done to their relationship. He hadn't told her that he loved Alice, but then she had not admitted to him that she'd stopped loving Alan long before his death.

She crossed the patio and started down the steps.

'Tell the pilot to wait.'

'Why?' she demanded. She forced herself not to turn back. She could not take much more of this...much more of him. She stared through the palms at a scrap of red that must be the helicopter.

She heard his step behind her, bare feet on the patio. She closed her eyes and it was as if he were there in front of her, dressed in trunks and nothing more. Angry and dangerous. She could feel the anger, could smell her own danger. She should run, but instead she froze, knowing she could never escape if he wanted to catch her.

He brushed past her, ignoring her gasp of protest. She watched his back moving towards the speck of red. The helicopter. She pressed her lips together, caught them with her teeth. Then she walked on towards the helicopter. She concentrated on stepping in the sand, walking on her toes, not sinking in with her heels.

He was back before she reached the end of the thatch of palm trees.

'He doesn't speak English,' Max muttered. 'I haven't a clue what he said.'

She stared at his chest. Anything but his eyes. In the middle of his chest there was a swirl of brown hair that had a tinge of red to it. The skin she could glimpse under his chest hair was not as darkly tanned as the rest of him. Under his trunks, would his flesh be paler? She flushed and jerked her eyes up.

'The pilot doesn't speak English.'

She should be able to talk to anyone without losing her cool. She'd learned that above all through her years in Peru. How to make graceful conversation no matter what was going on in her mind. He was in her path, in her way, not letting her go to the helicopter. 'It's waiting for me,' she said finally, her voice stiff.

'I told him ten minutes.'

She chewed on her lower lip, staring at his mouth, the harshness of his lips pressed thin. Why didn't he simply let her go, then it would be over? 'I thought you said he didn't speak English.'

'I got my meaning across. He said something about *prisa*.'

'Did he sound anxious?' she asked. How could they be talking linguistics when she would never see him again?

'Fatalistic. He sounded resigned.'

'*No tengo de prisa*. That's what he probably said. There's no hurry.' How could they be talking about the pilot when it was goodbye? Why didn't he simply let her go?

His jaw jerked. 'I live on a ranch, miles away from the city.'

She shifted her gaze to his chin. It was firm and broad, the sign of a strong man who liked his own way. 'I know you do.'

'I've no intention of moving to the city.'

'No,' she agreed. What was he talking about?

Her agreement seemed only to increase his belligerence. 'We get snow in the winter,' he growled. 'Have you ever seen snow?'

'Yes. In the mountains in Peru.' He looked sceptical and she added, 'From an airplane.' She didn't know what this conversation was about, but she could not walk away, not even with the memory of that hellish plane crash pushing through.

'The nearest neighbour is four miles away. That's Juan. There's a village of three hundred five miles in the other direction. Then there's the town. Williams Lake. It's forty miles, and you won't find the kind of clothes you're wearing today.'

Her breath packed up in her throat. 'What are you saying?'

He let out an explosive sigh. 'It would never work. You've no idea what you're getting into.'

She was afraid to look any higher than his chin. Terrified, because if he did not mean what he seemed to mean she had to be able to walk away, at least as far as that helicopter. She gulped. 'If other women manage, so can I.'

That muscle in his jaw jerked again. 'You can't even imagine the thought of living alone without a husband. There will be times you'll be screaming for a city. There's no theatre closer than Williams Lake. The biggest social event of the year is the stampede. You're accustomed to formal dances and maids and—have you ever cleaned a house?'

She lifted her eyes to his. 'Does cleaning an orphanage count?'

For seconds, he stared back into her eyes. 'Why, Faith? Why me?'

She saw that he needed a reason. A real reason. She swallowed twice, then said on a whisper, 'You'd be a good father for my child.'

His eyelids dropped. 'Better than Jorge?'

'Yes,' she agreed, hoping she could hold out until this test was over. It *was* a test, his eyes studying her as he questioned. She stared at his harsh face and knew he was trying to tell her forcefully how impossible it was. And she could not imagine any length of time wiping the image of this man's face from her heart.

'A better substitute for Alan?' he asked, his voice deliberately cruel.

She blinked, but that was the only sign she gave him that his barb had found her. For a moment, she had thought... She knew it was insane. Her impulse to suggest marriage had been craziness born of desperation. She'd only done it because it had seemed something bigger than herself was pushing her, telling her to trust the moment. A wild impulse, the sort she could imagine Cathy having. She wished she had Cathy's certainty, Cathy's knowledge of her own heart, her courage. For a moment last night, then again on the stairs just now, she'd believed the gamble was hers to take.

Just now, she had believed he wanted it too.

An illusion. In a moment she would leave. Back to Peru, to tell Jorge and her uncles that she was not going to be the co-operative woman they expected. Afterwards, she would go back to the village in Spain. It was easier to be alone there, looking after the babies.

'It's time for me to go, ' she said tonelessly.

'Not yet.' He placed himself firmly in her path. 'We'll be married in Mérida.'

* * *

A legal marriage, not a church ceremony. She had not been prepared for that, although she should have known.

The ceremony took place in a register office in Mérida. It was Mexico and Max did not speak Spanish, so Faith acted as translator. The licence. The gold bands he purchased for their fingers from a jeweller in the city. The ceremony. And when she held her hand out she gasped silently because she had forgotten to take Alan's ring off. She jerked it off and Max took it from her without a word, dropping it in his pocket. Then they exchanged rings, circles of gold pressed awkwardly on to stiff fingers.

Then the marriage certificate, formal words in Spanish. Max glanced at the paper that recorded their bonding and said indifferently, 'You keep it.' As if the paper meant nothing to him.

Married in haste in the heat of a Mérida afternoon.

She had made a terrible mistake.

Marry in haste. Repent at leisure. Faith could remember her mother saying that, talking about a neighbour in Seattle. She had remembered it again, clearly, after she married Alan—not at once, but when she'd understood that he had not married her for love or even desire.

Max hailed a taxi in the street outside the register office. Faith sat in the back seat, listening while Max and the driver communicated in a mixture of English and Spanish. Earlier, he had sent their bags to the El Presidente hotel. Now they would join their bags.

Their hotel room...

They were man and wife now, although Max had not touched her since that brief ceremony. 'Are you going to call your family?' he asked now. 'Or wire them?'

'I—I don't know.' She bit her lip. Her uncles were not going to be pleased. 'It's not the first time I've foiled their matrimonial plans for me,' she worried. Her attempt at a smile died when he did not return it.

'You want me to tell them for you?' He made the offer grimly, as if he would resent performing that service for her.

'I'll call them,' she said tightly. Not a church wedding. She could not tell them that. 'Maybe I'll wire them,' she decided. 'I'd better do it right away. I was supposed to be on a flight into Lima...' She stole a glance at him. He was frowning, not looking at her. 'Tomorrow afternoon,' she finished faintly.

'I'm sure you can send a telegram from the hotel.' He sounded as if he were talking to a stranger. He looked like a stranger, dressed in immaculate trousers and a white shirt open at the neck in concession to the heat. Until now, she had only known him in jeans and a bathing-suit. She didn't really know him at all. She tangled her fingers together in her lap. They *were* strangers.

At El Presidente, the manager of the hotel showed Faith to a quiet study where she could compose her telegrams while Max went off on some errand. He didn't tell her what he was doing, or where he was going. 'I'll see you in our room later,' was all he said.

She stared down at the blank telegraph form.

Their room. Later.

What on earth could she say to the uncles?

She pushed the form aside. The manager in the next room must have had radar, because he hurried to her side when she stood. He personally put through the long distance call for her, but there was no answer at Cathy and Juan's San Francisco home. Faith sighed and went back to the telegraph form. Cathy and Juan must be in Brazil still. Just as well. Getting Juan to break the news to the family could have had its drawbacks. Juan himself would want assurance that Faith had not made a terrible mistake.

And at this moment she could not give that assurance.

In the end she wrote the bare announcement on the telegraph form. Faith Corsica had married, would be returning to Canada with her new husband. She would contact the uncles with an address once she was settled in her new home.

Mercifully, she would miss the reaction to that telegram. She sent another to Cathy and Juan, announcing that her new husband was Juan's friend Max Davidson. She wondered if Cathy had told Juan about sending Faith to the island. What would Cathy think of *this* development? As for Juan—whatever reservations Juan might have about her hasty marriage, he would at least be able to reassure the uncles as to the character of her new husband.

The manager promised to dispatch the telegrams at once. With Latin courtesy, he did not look at the words she had written in her message. Instead, he personally escorted her to her room. To Max's room.

She unpacked her bag. The manager had agreed to retrieve the cases she had left at the Mérida airport, city clothes she'd known she would not need on Isla Catalina.

Max had not returned when her other luggage arrived from the airport. She unpacked the smaller case, called the desk and asked for a maid to press two of her suits. No point in unpacking the rest of her cases here. She'd been dragging her personal possessions along ever since Spain. She didn't know when she and Max would leave Mérida, but she suspected Max would want to get home to his ranch as soon as possible.

They weren't going to have a honeymoon. They were married, but no one could mistake Max for a proud and happy bridegroom.

Her gaze kept going to the big bed. One bed, and she wasn't sure which was the stronger emotion—nervousness, or that flush that thinking of his kiss always brought. She turned away impatiently and hovered over Max's suitcase, then decided he might be annoyed if she unpacked it.

At seven, Faith decided to go down to supper alone.

A massive mistake, marrying a man when all she knew was that he was a good companion on a tropical island, that when he touched her her pulse went wild. Back on Isla Catalina, it had seemed reasonable. Or perhaps it had been the wine talking when she'd offered to marry him. She didn't think he'd had much of the wine himself, but in the end he'd agreed to this insanity.

He'd gone out on some necessary errand and would be back soon. And somehow, they would make a marriage of it. Not for love, not like Cathy and Juan, but surely they could be friends? And she *would* be a good wife to him. She would!

The dining-room was quiet and dimly lit. The waiter arrived with a flourish, his eyes appreciative of the *señora*. She ordered the sort of meal she might have had in Lima. When she was halfway through the soup, the maître d' guided Max to her table and seated him.

'I wasn't sure when you'd be back,' she explained. She couldn't tell from his expression whether he was annoyed with her for coming down to the dining-room without waiting for him.

'I was organising our flight home,' he explained, adding for the waiter, *'Cerveza, por favor.'*

'I see you know how to do the basics in Spanish.'

'How to order a beer? Yes.'

It was going to be all right. He was smiling now, and he'd been organising their flight home. *Ours*, he had said. Not *mine*. Surely if he was thinking of them as a couple already, everything would work out?

'When are we leaving?'

'Tomorrow morning. We lay over in Denver overnight.'

'Denver?'

He shrugged and picked up the glass of beer the waiter had delivered to his place. 'I had to take what I could get to get us home at such short notice.' He glanced at the menu. 'What's that you're having?'

'*Sopa*—soup. I've ordered...'

'I'll have the same.' He made a gesture which the waiter evidently understood.

'You might not like it,' she warned. 'It's quite *picante*.' He raised his brows and she translated, 'Spicy.'

'I'll trust your taste. I've eaten better this last week than I can ever remember.'

For some reason, the compliment had the effect of depressing her. She bent over her soup and lifted the spoon.

'There's a ton of luggage in our room,' Max said mildly.

'I had my bags sent over from the airport.' She ate another spoonful of the soup. 'I left some things there last week.'

'The maid brought some stuff on hangers as well.' His eyes surveyed what he could see of the silk suit she was wearing. 'While we're in Denver, we'd better get you some clothes.'

'But I've——'

'The jeans you borrowed from Cathy are what you'll need. You can't wear silk and lace for everyday life on a ranch.' His eyes narrowed. 'Also,' he reminded her, 'there's no maid at Shady Mountain Ranch. My foreman's wife sometimes cooks the odd meal and there's a woman who comes to do the cleaning twice a week. Other than that you'll be on your own.'

'I'll be fine.' What did he mean when he said she would be on her own? As if he would not be around at all. 'What's her name?'

'Who?'

'Your foreman's wife.' How many women were there in his life?

'Sarah. She does my books too.'

'Yes, you told me that before.' Faith was relieved at the thought that the foreman's wife was another woman who, even if she did not live on the ranch, would be there most days. Faith had had time in the last few hours to realise that she had no idea what a Canadian ranch was like. She was accustomed to the company of other women, both in Spain and in Peru. To be isolated on a big tract of land with only men around had the potential for real loneliness. Especially when her husband did not love her.

'Does Sarah live on the ranch?' she asked.

'Yes.' He was slowly turning his glass in his hands. 'The foreman has a house down the hill from the ranch house. Look, Faith...'

'Does Alice live... near by?'

'In the village. Why?'

She put the spoon down into her bowl. 'I just wondered.'

'You will see her.' He held her eyes. 'It's a small ranching community. When there's a social gathering, everyone in the area gets invited.'

'I understand.'

'Does that bother you?' He would not let her eyes free. 'Seeing Alice?'

'Yes.' He had known Alice better than he knew Faith. She drew in a deep breath. 'But I'll make sure no one realises that it bothers me.' She felt a lump rising in her throat and was shocked to realise it was anger. She fought it down and said in a neutral voice, 'And if we're having a social gathering and it's appropriate, I'll invite her.'

He stared at her for a long time, without words. 'Max...'

He put down his empty glass. 'As for Sarah, my foreman's wife...'

She shivered at the look in his eyes. Fierce.

'You'd best be prepared.'

'Prepared?' she echoed.

'I don't want you making her feel uncomfortable.'

'Why would I...?'

'She's confined to a wheelchair.'

'I—of course I won't do anything to make her feel uncomfortable.' Did he think she would react so badly as to make a handicapped woman feel uncomfortable in her presence? 'What happened to her?'

'A car accident, five years ago.'

CHAPTER SEVEN

MAX leaned back to allow the waiter to place his soup on the table. Across from him, Faith was playing with her spoon, pretending to eat. She was obviously nervous.

Hell, so was he! They both had a right to it. If he had any sense, he'd put her on the first jet to South America, unwrap that ridiculous wedding ceremony. Except that he supposed divorce would not be an option for a good Catholic woman like Faith—or did the fact that it had not been a church ceremony make a difference?

His wife.

What he should do was call Juan. Knowing Juan Corsica, Max was certain the Peruvian would know how to undo an unconsummated Mexican marriage. Juan would also be very angry—Max would be, in his place. The last thing he would want to hear would be Max's real reason for marrying Faith. Anger was the closest thing he had to an excuse. He had married Faith to stop her marrying a man whose only power over her seemed to be an ability to turn her voice uneasy when she said his name. When Max thought of Faith giving herself away for security and the chance to have a child...

His jaw clenched as he admitted the other reason. From the first time he'd seen Faith, he had wanted her with an uncomfortable insistence. Lust, and it only grew stronger, although he had told himself he would be free of her when she left the island.

Then she had ruined it all with that ridiculous proposal. *'You could marry me.'*

Ridiculous! Except that he had lain awake all night, knowing from the memory of the tremor on her flesh that he could have persuaded her to give herself to him without the wedding-ring. Knowing that he *could* not... but the little voice echoing in his mind, reminding him that her lips had been hot, sweet honey under his, her breathing ragged and her body soft and willing.

If he married her...

Of course it was insane. He'd lost his head, let his desire swamp his brain like a damned teenager. Fool! He'd never been a rash man, always thought before he acted. Until this morning, when he'd truly lost all grip on reason. He remembered the swing of her hip as she walked past him on her way to the helicopter, the way her walk had become more sensual with the high heels she was wearing. He remembered the silk on her body and her legs and that helicopter outside, waiting to take her away. And yet he'd known that if he reached for her, he could have her.

All right. So he'd made a mess for himself. The worst of it was that, given the chance to go back a few hours, he would probably make the same decision again. It made no sense at all, but it was impossible to let her walk away.

All right. They were married. He'd make the best of it.

Her fingers were torturing the spoon. Was she dreading later, upstairs in their room? She had been soft in his arms back on the island, soft and heated and breathless. Had it been an act? A part of the sacrifice? Pretence? Bait?

Max knew he did not understand the culture she came from, knew that the world she had lived in was very different, the rules more important. He knew that those same cultural differences had kept Juan Corsica away from the woman he loved for fourteen years. And any fool could see that Juan was nuts about Cathy. It took a lot of love to make a cross-culture marriage work.

He sighed.

Faith jerked.

What was she thinking? Was she worried? Frightened?

She should be terrified. She had just married a man she did not know. She was about to go to live in a strange country. What did a man do with a wife he had not asked for, a woman still obsessed by a dead husband? She'd worn Alan's ring to her wedding ceremony. He must always remember that. Easy to forget, to think of the way she was in his arms. It was two years since she'd been widowed, but she still came apart when she talked about her husband. He must not forget when he felt a sigh from her lips that she was probably deep in another passion. Another man.

A man had to be crazy to get into this position. Even crazier to feel his pulse hammering when she caught her lower lip between her teeth...when she took in a deep breath and her breasts swelled against the silk of her blouse.

Upstairs was one bed, one room. She was no trembling virgin. She knew marriage meant sharing that bed with him.

Last night, standing on the beach, she would have given him a sample of the merchandise. If he'd wanted. He picked up the spoon and dipped it into his own soup and wondered what the hell it was he wanted out of this set-up. He'd never before in his life been trapped in such a ridiculous situation. He still did not understand why he could not let her go back to Peru and struggle with her fate alone. Sure, he wanted her, but he had wanted other women in his thirty-eight years. He had not reached for all the women he'd felt desire for. Not even most of them. And this one—he had recognised that she was trouble from the moment he'd seen her scantily dressed body hurrying towards him on the beach.

He knew better. He'd been old enough to see what happened to his father, the consequences of reaching for someone who did not fit in the world of a rancher. He'd known better than to repeat that mistake. When Alice showed her true colours, he'd ended their relationship immediately. Yet now in the space of a single morning he'd taken on a woman he lusted after and did not understand. A woman obsessed with a ghost. A woman from a world Cathy had once said laughingly was filled with servants and disapproval.

Max Davidson had always avoided the kind of action that brought regrets. Until now. How in hell could Faith ever fit into his life?

If anyone had told him when he left Canada for a Mexican holiday that he'd return with a wife, he would have said they were crazy. And if he'd believed that he would actually marry a woman he'd only kissed once, a woman who would wear her dead husband's ring to their wedding...

Upstairs, the bed was waiting for them.

Across the table was his wife, her dark hair passionately abundant, her eyes wary. If she called out her husband's name when he was buried deep in her, he might throttle her with his bare hands. He had never in his life touched a woman when there was violence in his heart, but this woman...

If he had any sense, he'd leave her alone in that bed upstairs.

If he had any sense.

Faith was apprehensive. Max was being courteous and considerate. He was answering all her questions about his home, telling her more about his sister Beth, who lived three miles away with her husband. About their three-year-old son named Jerry and the baby due soon.

With every word Max said, she could feel how foreign his world was. She did not belong, would not belong. It might have been different if he had brought her home as his love and his bride. With a man who loved her at her side, she could have become one of the family. But she was a stranger, a foreigner.

Once again she had married to a man who did not love her. Perhaps he didn't even want her. Oh, she knew that he desired her physically, but he did not want her in his life. He was talking, polite, but his eyes were wary and she knew she did not have his full attention. He was regretting it, already sorry.

No wonder. A stupid woman. That's what she was.

A group of musicians were serenading a couple on the far side of the room. Max asked her to translate the song.

'It's a love song,' she told him uneasily.

There was an outburst of conversation and laughter from the table. Max lifted his brow in a question.

'They're celebrating their anniversary.' Her mouth felt stiff. 'They've been married seven years.' What would happen to this marriage in seven years? Seven months?

When the musicians retreated to the microphones at the end of the room, the celebrating couple got up to dance. After a moment they were joined by two more couples from further back in the room.

'Dance?' asked Max.

'Está bien,' she replied, not realising she had answered in Spanish until he frowned. 'OK,' she added hurriedly, standing when he did. Did he disapprove of her speaking Spanish? She had grown up between two cultures. Most of her relatives in Peru spoke English and Spanish with equal fluency. Must she now learn to monitor her speech?

She walked at his side to the dance-floor, aware of his height in a way she had not been previously. She was tall for a Latin girl, not much more than average for an American. But Alan had not been a tall man, and the men she had danced with at balls in Lima tended to be not much taller than her. Latin men.

She turned towards her husband, suddenly wary of his height, his breadth. A big man. Her gaze travelled from his eyes, down to his shoulders. She felt a tingle of fear that was half excitement. When he touched her...

She was trembling, although he was moving formally, without fault, guiding her to the music. His touch on her waist was impersonal.

'You're a good dancer,' she murmured. She had been trained to make interesting and flattering conversation with any man, but in this moment she could think of nothing more to say to him. For all the intimacy of his touch on her, she might have been his maiden aunt.

He smiled, but she was watching his eyes, her head tipped back, and there was no laughter there at all. 'I had a sadist for a teacher in grade nine,' he explained. 'She insisted we boys all learn to handle ourselves on the dance-floor. Ballroom dancing, although there's not much of that in my part of the world.'

What did they do in British Columbia? If they didn't dance...? Faith bit her lip, uncomfortably aware that her knowledge of current North American social habits was badly lacking. When she'd come north on trips with Alan, she'd never been involved in any social life to speak of. It had been years—twelve years—since she'd been a young woman spending the summer with her American aunt.

'You don't dance in British Columbia?' Her fingers were curled around his hand, as if she were clasping it. She made them go slack.

'The kids do, at least they call it dancing. And there's a square-dance group that gets together in the village. When there's a party, of course we do dance, but perhaps not with the formal enthusiasm they do here.' He nodded his head towards the couple putting on an impressive exhibition of the tango on the other side of the dancefloor.

She managed to reply lightly, thankful for the years of training she had in not letting her inner distress show. Not that she needed dancing to live, but she knew nothing about square dancing except for when she'd once seen a group of eight men and women on television. The women had been dressed in matching swirling skirts. They had moved with confidence in response to the instructions of a man calling out incomprehensible commands through a microphone.

Would he expect her to know how to square dance? She would have to find a book, study the moves in secret.

From his conversation, she knew that he had a large property. He would be a leader in the community. The wife of such a man would be expected to entertain. She was beginning to realise that the rules would all be different. What kind of entertaining would she be expected to do?

When the dance was over, he did not suggest another. Had he handled Alice this impersonally on the dancefloor?

'We may as well go up,' he decided.

Faith nodded, although by Latin standards it was early yet. Upstairs the bed was waiting for them. One big bed, and tonight he would sleep in it with her. There was no point in trying to put that moment off, although Faith wished now that he had made love to her back on the island. *Anything* to avoid this awkwardness. If he had made love to her last night when she'd felt his need, her pulse heavy between them...

If only she had not interrupted with her suggestion of marriage, it might have happened then. It would be easier now if they had already been intimate. She stood beside him in the lift, staring at the doors that slid closed. Shutting them in together. Alone. Up on the fourth floor, the bedroom they would share was waiting.

Max cleared his throat as the lift lurched into motion. 'You don't have to worry.'

'What?' What did he mean? Could he read her mind?

He was staring at the panel of control buttons for the lift. 'We should give it some time,' he said, and she saw a muscle jerk in his throat. 'We may be sharing the same bed, but I think we should wait to... to consummate the marriage. Until... give it time. We should give it time.'

Maybe it was relief she felt, but she knew this was a bad idea. Waiting would only create tension between them. There was already this uncomfortable distance—half a metre between them and it felt like half a kilometre. Alan hadn't loved her, but she had *believed* that he did. That had made it easier. But this... She felt like a commodity, a wife on approval. And she felt completely... confused.

Didn't he want to make love to her? The only thing she *was* sure of was that she had got herself into a mess. She had made a big mistake, but lying silently in bed beside a man she belonged to but did not understand would not do anything to make things right.

He opened the door to their room without speaking, held it for her to go in. She heard the snap of the latch closing them in, then felt rather than heard as he crossed the room to his suitcase. 'I'm having a shower,' he announced. 'Unless you...?'

She shook her head, staring at the big bed, not meeting his eyes. 'I showered before I went to dinner.'

'Right, then.' He disappeared into the bathroom.

She undressed quickly, aware that he might open the door at any moment, might come back into the room and find her dressed only in her underwear. It would not be the first time he'd seen her that way, but with the walls of this bedroom surrounding them she could not stand in his gaze without trembling.

She would be asleep before he finished his shower. When he came to bed, she would be turned away from him, sleeping—well, pretending to sleep. Then, eventually, his breathing would deepen and she would only have to get through the night. In a novel, the heroine would fall asleep and wake up entangled in the hero's arms. What if sleep seduced her into his arms? What if the pulsing weakness she had felt last night in his arms slipped into her dreams?

She *must* not sleep!

Back at the ranch, at his home—would she be sharing a room with him? A bed? In Lima, she and Alan had had separate rooms. After a while, he had not come to her very often. In the end, it was a wonder she'd managed to become pregnant, although she had been so excited, so hungry for the child to come, to lie in her arms with eyes closed and tiny mouth parted.

Oh, God! She mustn't cry! She mustn't.

Was there any chance at all that this marriage could work? She knew that Max was not a man who would love her passionately. She could see the need for control in him, knew he did not desire that kind of love for himself. Well, she was accustomed to that. She could care for him, be a friend and a good wife to him. If she had his respect and his friendship, it might work. Many marriages in Peru were built on less than friendship. Once she had yearned for a true, passionate love that came from deep in the heart. She had learned to expect less, to be content with less.

She closed her eyes, sinking down on the side of the bed, her hand pressed to her face, feeling the flush of distress there. She had dreamed ... oh, she knew it could not happen, but last night, with his desire thick on the air and his eyes searching hungrily through the darkness of an island night, she had dreamed that she could reach out and touch his cheek with her hand, that he would give a sigh that was half-groan and all love. That she could whisper a confession of love to him and she would be the only woman he had ever wanted.

He had never said anything to make her believe that he might come to feel love for her. She'd had no reason to expect anything like that. She'd been a crazy dreamer, a stupid young girl to think that if he married her she could teach him to love her. She had no skills to draw love from any man. No courage to try.

Come morning, they would be busy, getting to the airport, flying to the States. What would happen the next day at the border to Canada? What kind of formality was involved for Max to bring his Peruvian-American wife into the country? What if they turned her back? Better, she supposed, if they didn't let her into the country. She would be forced back to the world where she belonged.

What if Max told her that he wanted this marriage ended? It could be... could be annulled. Nothing had happened. They had exchanged legal vows, but in the lift he had made it clear that he had no intention of exercising the rights he'd gained over her. What if he told her to leave him, to go back home? She—it made no sense at all, but she did not want to go! She wanted to stay, to use every minute she had to try to make him care for her as he must have cared for Alice.

Had he loved Alice?

Did he still love her?

Faith pulled on a satin nightgown that buttoned high on to her throat. Not that he would see anything. She would be hidden under the blankets and he was not going to look. Wait, he had said. Wait for what? Despite last night, perhaps he did not want her at all. Had he married her only to prevent her messing up her life by marrying Jorge?

No man was that altruistic.

She got under the covers on the far side of the bed. The light was still on. He would be able to see her shape through the blankets when he came into the room from his shower. She closed her eyes and was shaken by an image that was pure fantasy, but her body clenched with tension because it was more than real. Max standing erect, his long body naked, the water in the shower flowing down over him. She'd seen him in a brief bathing-suit and her imagination supplied the rest. With the water rushing over his sun-darkened skin, the image hot in her imagination, she began to tremble and she felt her hand go out to touch the wet curls on his chest.

She touched nothing. She clenched her fingers. As if he were real. As if she were there in the shower with him.

Oh, God! This was terrible. Frightening, because she'd never felt anything like this before. This wild curiosity, stirred and stirring and pulsing along her veins. She remembered the muscle that had clenched deep inside her when he'd said she need not be afraid. She *had* been nervous. That side of marriage had been sharply disappointing to her. *She* had been disappointing to her husband and that could well happen again in this marriage. Thinking of this night and this bed, she had feared that she would be too inexperienced for Max, because her marriage to Alan wasn't experience at all. Just disappointment on both sides, except he'd got the factory he wanted.

She was going to disappoint Max. She knew that her body hinted at voluptuousness. When the time came, he would expect a passion from her that she was not capable of. Although when he kissed her...she wished...she yearned for her body to be hot and pleasing to him.

He didn't even want her enough to make love to her on their wedding night.

She was about to get out of the bed to turn the light off when she heard the sound on the other side of the bathroom door. He was coming into the room! She turned away to face the wall. On the wall she could see a cockroach. As she watched, it ran down towards the floor—a reminder that she was in Mexico. At home in Peru there were not nearly so many of them.

The door opened. Tension jerked into her body. She forced herself to breathe very slowly, to relax. She wanted to look as a woman might if she truly were sleeping with her face turned away from the man who had just entered the room.

Her husband.

At home in Peru...

It was not her home any longer. Her new home was a country she had never seen. She'd travelled much of the world in her life, but she was going among strangers now. She blinked and blinked again, but the tears slipped out. She dared not reach to brush them away. Whatever happened, he must not see her cry.

The light went out suddenly. Darkness. She could see a square of light from the draped window. Street-lights outside. Sounds from the open window. Mérida was not ready for bed yet.

The mattress shifted as it took his weight. She caught her lip between her teeth to bite off the gasp. She felt the movement of air. He was getting under the blankets. Could she stay awake all night? With his weight on the other side of the bed, the mattress was sloped slightly towards him. She might roll against him and he would think she was coming to him in the night, begging for his caress, for his murmur of desire against her skin.

She had to stop this! Images, wild in her mind. Yearning, and she'd never felt like this before. Frightened that he would touch her, aching because he had told her he would not.

'Faith?'

She sucked in a slow breath. 'Yes?'

He touched her shoulder, a light brush of his fingers on the satin of her gown. She shivered and turned to face him. She found his shape in the dark with her eyes. Mercifully, the darkness hid the drying tears on her cheeks.

'We're going to try to make this thing work.'

'Yes,' she agreed on a whisper. Her heart was pounding.

His hand brushed her face. Her lips parted on a surprise, but no sound came. His caress was light, tentative against the ivory of her cheek. Then his fingers stilled.

'You've been crying.'

'I—I didn't mean to.'

His touch softened, tracing the dampness on her cheek. 'Why, Faith? What are you crying for...?'

'Because...' She closed her eyes, felt his fingers brush her eyelashes, her own pulse throbbing. She trembled and his touch stilled.

'Are you afraid of me?'

She was afraid he would never love her. Afraid this pulsing in her body would go on forever and desire would swamp her because she had no knowledge of how to cope with what he did to her body.

'Are you?' he demanded, his voice hardening. 'You needn't fear me.'

'I'm... I don't know why—why you married me.' She squeezed her eyes closed, shaken because she could hear the pleading in her own voice. She had to control that! She must *never* let herself beg for his love!

'I don't really know why either.' His hand cupped the side of her face. 'Perhaps because you asked. Because...' Her eyes flew open, but there was nothing to see, only the fact that he was close. She trapped her lip between her teeth to stop the trembling. She could smell the soap he had used in his shower, the dampness that must lie in his hair. She reached and her fingers found his shoulder. It seemed as if his flesh trembled at her touch. Tentatively, she moved her fingers in a caress of the still-damp skin.

'Damn it, Faith! This is...'

'Don't you want to?' she whispered. Dark. So dark. She heard the bed protest as he moved. Then his hand moved to the side of her throat and she saw his head moving closer. In silhouette his mouth moved to cover hers. Her lips trembled as they touched.

'Damn you,' he growled softly as his mouth settled over hers.

'Max...' A whisper, touching his kiss.

'It's no good,' he groaned and his hand slid to her shoulder.

He teased her mouth open, his tongue urging softly against her tightly pressed lips. She sighed. Her lips parted and he entered. His fingers caressed along the satin of her gown, his thumb dipping into the softness at the hollow of her shoulder through the seductive slipperiness of the fabric. Muted by satin, his touch drew a whisper from her lips.

He deepened the kiss.

Her eyes closed, her body softening, pressing closer to the urging of his lips and his hands. She felt his fingers on the buttons that closed her gown at the throat. Her breath stopped.

'Faith?'

Somewhere outside, a man laughed. A woman said something in reply.

Faith could feel the backs of Max's fingers brushing her flesh. One button free, perhaps two. She clung to the numbers, feeling the surge of sensation welling up inside her. Something frightening, sensation filled with emotion threatening to explode out of her control. She whimpered. She heard the sound and it was too late to pull it back.

He answered, a low groan at the back of his throat.

Sensations everywhere. Places he touched, others where his hand and his mouth had not reached, but something wild in her was aching, yearning, and it was that wild need that made the sounds escape her throat as his hands moved over her, arousing and confident on her gown in the dark.

He was very good at this. Experienced. The sound whispered out of her lungs and he heard, paused, and his hand returned to the place he'd just touched. The fabric between them only stirred the flames that surged over her flesh ahead of his touch. She felt him change his caress when her breathing altered. She felt conscious and somehow used, but she could not hold back the response, and the sensations turned to fear, because she could feel her control slipping away and she wanted it to leave her entirely and he was watching, knowing, and although his body was hard and full of need against her he knew what pulsed in her and he controlled it, playing her nerves as a master would a sensitive instrument.

A shock of sensation knifed through her, clutching at the heart of her woman's body. His hand, cupped against her naked breast. His kiss penetrated deeper, smothering her gasp, taking it inside him, and maybe it was sound outside, or perhaps the sea ringing in her ears, the man touching, bending his mouth to take her nipple between his lips, and her cry, and his hand sliding along the satin over her thigh, then finding the flesh underneath, and she moaned or he did, and the words were pounding in her blood and it was the only thing she knew—that she must not say them.

I love you. Oh, God, I love you so and I can't and I don't know...

He swept the gown up and his hand was on her thigh, her hip, her belly. 'Faith...' His voice was a low growl of possession. Then he touched her and she heard the cry and she was begging for love and she must not say the words, must bite her lips and keep the words in and tell him only with her hands, restless, needing, touching ... but it was lost, gone and she could not ... She cried out and his body answered and it was all flames and if he touched her *there* she would ... oh, please! Please!

Words on her mind. Pleas and whispers and the sounds and the needs were all mixed together and she only knew it was burning ... burning and if he did ... didn't ... please ... touch ... love ... can't ... have to ...

'Faith...'

His heart was under her palm and then she was crushed into him and he moved hungrily and he found the place that made her cry out and she tried to bury her mouth against his throat or she might say anything, everything. 'I—oh ... I ... please ... please ...' She buried her husky voice against the musky dampness of his heated flesh.

He nestled his face between her breasts, turned and drew one nipple deep inside, and she knew that he meant her to cry out with need and that she must not let her body forget reason, but he fondled the peak of her breast with his tongue and her body betrayed her, clutched him, and she whimpered, moaned, and if the words were going to come out they would come.

He'd pulled her gown away slowly and as the satin crawled up her body she whimpered with aching and heat. Then he tossed it aside and touched the length of her body with his and her flesh was restless and hungry and a female instinct she had not previously been aware of was inside her, knowing how to move, to stir the need in him, because if he did not take her, fill her hunger, she would die with aching frustration.

Then he was still.

His hands on her. His body tangled with hers. Naked, tangled together.

'Faith...'

Her body moved with urgency. He sounded so...harsh. His hands on her, his mouth...but her name on his lips was grim, demanding.

'What?' she whispered. He could not pull away from her, leave her like *this*! She'd never...could not bear...

'I want you to say...'

'What?' She would say anything! Anything!

He bent as if he was going to touch her breast again, draw her need into his kiss. She moaned and moved under him, but the kiss did not come. Her body clutched at him. 'Please,' she begged on a whisper, a thread of need. 'Please...say what? Anything...'

'Nothing.' His body moved over hers and his voice was a harsh thread of desperation. 'Say nothing.'

She felt her insides pulsing with fire. She touched his chest, drawing her fingers over the contours, finding the hard nub of his nipple through the curls of his chest hair. His body jerked and she pulled herself up to him with strong, desperate arms, burying her mouth in his chest and seeking his nipple with her tongue and tiny nips of her teeth, and when she found her goal he gasped and she knew that she had power too and moved against him and touched and kissed and bit with teeth and he pushed her away, down, and he was coming down over her and the breath was harsh and loud, tearing through his lungs, and the heat was intense, too much, burning, swamping, and she was frightened and buried in the flames, and it was not fear but a cry of surrender, taking, urging, pulling him down and sliding her hand along the hard tension of his chest, his abdomen, the tangle of heat and sensation.

'Damn you,' he groaned as he buried himself in her, and she felt the pain of his voice cursing her, felt the exaltation of her body possessing him. He buried her cry with his mouth and she burned in the flames he drove to consume them both.

CHAPTER EIGHT

THERE were shadows in the valley when Faith and Max arrived home.

Max had glanced at her several times during the flight from Denver to Vancouver. They were flying in a big jet and she was usually not too bad if she didn't have to look out and *see* how far above the earth she was. But Max had given her the window-seat and she kept finding herself turning her head, looking down. She tried to talk, making conversation to mask her tension. She knew that Max already thought her ridiculously sheltered. By Canadian standards she obviously was. A world traveller, but a woman of thirty-one who had never lived outside the shadow of her own family. She didn't want to add to his poor opinion by letting him see how uneasy she was in the air. Hopelessly naïve and a coward as well.

She flushed, turning away from Max's curious glance. Naïve? She had been naïve in the ways of loving before she married him, but after the last three nights... Max's touch and his body were teaching her that flames were only a cool shadow beside what happened when he stroked her. It was getting worse. Sometimes she felt the heat when he was not even in the same room. Her flesh remembered and the wild ache came on her when there was no reason, when she was brushing her teeth or changing into new jeans in a department store in the middle of Denver.

She wanted to cling to him, but he felt no need to keep her near when the night was over. That afternoon in

Denver he had sent her out shopping and said only that he had an appointment. She understood that he did not care to be questioned about his movements. An appointment, and she had learned during those years with Alan not to ask. Not her business. But in the changing-room of the department store, standing in her brief bikini panties and catching a glimpse of her long legs in the mirror...

She had felt the flush of desire crawl over her, the knowledge that, although they might be strangers in the daylight, in darkness he would come to her and she would have the power to make him groan her name and flame into need. He needed her then.

It was a double trap, because her need was greater. When daylight came, Max rose from the hotel beds they shared, and the man who had loved her through the night was gone. She often remembered how he had cursed her the first time they made love. She knew what that curse meant. He would have preferred their loving to be without the wildness she stirred in him. When she touched him in ways that drove the control from him, she felt a primitive sense of victory followed by the dry nausea of disappointment, because she knew he resented the power their passion had over him. He made sure it was a limited power, never escaping into the daytime world.

She was the one in the trap, exposed to him if he looked for the clues. She was trapped in both love and passion. It would not have mattered when or where. If he said, 'Come,' she would drop anything and follow him to the ends of the earth.

She *was* following him to the ends of the earth, although if she had known the depth of her danger she might have hesitated, fearful of being destroyed, because, although she had whispered love to herself, she had not understood that her body could become the slave of its own needs.

Her vision cleared and she gulped, suddenly aware that she was staring down on a nasty-looking range of mountains. She felt the dizziness and her vision glazed. Snow and mountains, and the little plane had tossed, and the air had been so thin, so high, and she'd been nauseous and afraid because they were so high, and what if the nausea meant some harm to the baby, and how could she have been such a fool as to have insisted on coming with Alan on this trip? What if it hurt the baby?

A last effort to save something from her marriage. She had known by then that there was not only the woman in Seattle, but also a mistress somewhere in Lima. With the child coming, she'd ached for a real loving family to greet her baby's birth.

'Faith?'

She jerked her eyes away from the memories. Those terrible peaks. She should not have survived, but she had. She had been the only one, and lucky because the emergency locator had gone off on the plane and help had come before it was too late.

'Faith? Are you all right?'

Max. Not the nightmare. Just high in the sky, remembering.

She gulped and nodded, her eyes clinging to him because she might look back out of that window and she would be lost again in the horror. This was no tiny, frail airplane. She was on a big, modern jet. Nothing like that other time. She wished she could grip Max's hand and let his strength flow into her.

'Yes,' she made herself say. 'I'm fine. When will we be in Vancouver?'

'Twenty minutes.' He picked up the magazine he'd been reading and was instantly buried in it again. She stared down at his magazine. He was reading an article about maximising beef yields without using chemicals. She'd been on the Corsica hacienda in Peru, but she knew nothing of the technical side of ranching. She would have to learn Max's world. She knew how to be an upper class Peruvian woman, living a sheltered existence. A *genta dorada*. A woman of the idle wealthy.

Could she be a Canadian rancher's wife?

Max turned a page. Faith stared at a picture of a dozen cows grazing in a field of hay. Her eyes flicked up to his face and she shivered. It was the face of a hard man. She was married to him and she had never been in such danger in her life. Her fingers ached to reach out and touch. A wisp of memory could turn her body to flames at any moment and she believed now that it would get worse, not better. Each day the need flared higher; each night her body grew more desperate for his loving.

What would happen to the hardness in his face if she reached out to touch his cheek right now? She gulped and swallowed and mercifully her voice was steady. 'Do the cows have names?' she asked.

He stared at her as if she'd lost her reason.

'Your cows, I mean.' She gulped. 'I just wondered if you name them.'

'Not usually.' Amusement had replaced the astonishment in his eyes and she felt some of her tension easing.

'Sometimes, then?'

'Occasionally one of them does something to earn a name.' He was smiling now and her lips curved in answer. 'Bessie, for example,' he said.

'What did Bessie do?' It was a relief to be able to look at him, to have a reason to keep her gaze away from the window and the mountains.

'Got hit by a truck.'

'Oh! Was she . . . ?'

'No, it didn't kill her, but it was a close thing.' He closed his magazine and turned slightly towards her, frowning with the memory. 'I operated and——'

'Operated?'

'I'm a licensed veterinary surgeon,' he explained. 'I practised as a vet before I took over the farm. I still do my own animals.'

So much she did not know about him.

'Bessie was pregnant and I felt sure we'd lose the calf and probably the cow as well. It was a long night.' His eyes held determination mixed with worry, the echo of that night. 'You spend that many hours fighting for a cow's life,' he explained with a self-conscious shrug, 'you've got to give her a name.'

'Of course,' she agreed softly. When they exchanged a smile she felt hope warming her. He had said they were going to try to make this work. Surely that meant he was willing to love her?

She turned to look out of the window. She'd been so deep in watching him talk about Bessie that she gasped when the reality hit her. Miles up in the sky, angry mountains down below.

'What is it?' he asked. 'Are you uncomfortable?'

'I... How far from Vancouver is your ranch?'

'About two hundred miles.'

'Miles?' she echoed, her eyes fastening on his face. His mouth curved slightly and she felt the fear ease in her chest again.

'I suppose Peru is metric?'

'Yes.'

'We're supposed to be in Canada, but some of us are resistant to the change. Say three hundred kilometres. That's as the crow flies. Further by road.'

'In Peru, we'd say "as the condor flies".' Roads were limited in Peru because of the mountains. If the mountains she'd just glimpsed out of the window were typical of British Columbia, it was hard to imagine there *could* be a road. Max was frowning and she asked uneasily, 'Do you mind me talking about Peru?'

'You don't have to please me with your conversation.' But he looked irritated and she vowed she'd try not to refer to Peru or speak Spanish in future. Because he did not love her, she must be very careful to please him as much as she could. If he loved her as Juan did Cathy, perhaps she would have the courage to be exactly herself and know that his love would embrace the person she really was.

'We'll transfer to my plane in Vancouver,' he announced idly.

'Your plane?'

'I've got a small Cessna I use to get around.'

'A small...' She gulped. 'Isn't there a road to your ranch?'

'Of course there's a road. Six hours' drive from Vancouver, if you'd prefer to drive. By plane it's less than two hours.' His voice told her that anyone would be crazy to prefer the road.

She would endure hours of mountain driving to avoid climbing into a tiny hunk of tin that flew over the peaks. 'Are there...?' She cleared her throat. 'Do we fly over any mountains between Vancouver and your home?'

'Hmm.' He was back in his cattle magazine, but he smiled slightly. 'I can't offer you twenty-thousand-foot summits like the Andes, but we fly over the Coast Mountains. If you're a mountain lover...' he looked up and she saw the most complete smile he had given her all day, and she tried to make her lips curve in response '...I think you'll find them worth while.'

'Is that...?' She gestured out of the window.

'Yes, the Coast Mountains, but of course we'll be flying much lower. You'll get a much better look at them.'

Oh, God!

She had no idea how she managed it. She supposed that a person could do almost anything if she had to. It was impossible to tell him she was terrified, but it took all the discipline she had learned in ten miserable years married to Alan. All that practice, standing at her husband's side at formal balls, smiling and making conversation and feeling Alan's hand at her back and knowing that he was probably counting the moments until he could escape, take her home and leave, go to his mistress.

At least she had not disappointed Max in the bedroom. Their three nights had been passion-filled, hot and wild, and she knew that when they were in bed together he was almost as out of control in their loving as she was. For him, though, it ended with the dawn. She supposed it was different for a man, but at least that part of their marriage seemed to be successful. Somehow she would make the rest a success. She wasn't going to disappoint him by cowering at the sight of a Cessna.

At Vancouver Airport she walked at his side to the little plane. She stood silently on the tarmac while Max supervised the stowing of their luggage in the luggage compartment, the overflow of her bags going into the back seat.

'Good thing we don't have passengers,' he said wryly. 'We'd never get off the ground with all your bags. They weigh a ton.'

She felt herself pale.

'What's wrong?' he demanded sharply. 'You look——'

'Nothing!' She forced a smile and thanked heaven when he turned away and she could let the stiff curve of her lips go slack.

'Hop in, then, and I'll do my pre-flight check.'

She stared at the door he opened. He was amused at her hesitation.

'Haven't you been in a small plane before? Just climb up there. Put your foot here.' He indicated the place and she scrambled up and sat with her hands clenched together while he closed the door and shut her in. Then he walked around the plane with a frown on his face and finally climbed up into the seat beside her.

'Is everything OK?' she asked uneasily.

'Yes, of course.' He was flicking buttons on the dashboard of the plane. 'We wouldn't take off if it weren't. You'd better do up your seatbelt.'

Two hours by plane. That was what he'd said. Surely she could manage it? She turned her wrist and his glance dropped down to her silver watch.

'You haven't set your watch back. We're one hour earlier than Denver.'

She concentrated on setting her watch to the new time zone while he started the engine. Three in the afternoon. They should be at the ranch by five. How high could she count in a hundred and twenty minutes? One ... two ... three ... How many seconds ... surely she could mask her fear so that he need not know?

If only she had a book to read she could make her eyes move over the words, avoid looking out through that windscreen. But she had no book with her, had not read anything since the wedding. These last three days she had been concentrating on only one thing: getting through the days, trying to guess what Max wanted of her, trying to be—trying to know what sort of wife he desired and be that person.

Three days of waiting for night to fall, feeling the flush flow across her skin whenever she was caught in a memory. She had never known she could be wanton, more than eager for the pleasures of the marriage bed. Remembering... With the heat came embarrassment and a vow to be more controlled this time, not to let herself lose every vestige of reserve and control. She always tried to hold the words back, knowing the danger if she told him of love, if she made him feel she was clinging emotionally. A man like Max would not want a clinging wife. He already thought she was weak-willed, letting her family pressure her towards a marriage.

So far, she had managed to keep herself from crying out his name and begging him to love her... to please love her, and telling him that she wanted to be his in more than her body and she loved him and ached to hear the words on his lips.

Love me. Please love me.

She had managed not to beg for his love, to keep those words inside. Each night he forced the sounds from her and sometimes she begged him to take her with sounds and moans and need. But if she ever let the words out she might not be able to stop the flood and he would turn from her.

I love you.

Please love me. Love all of me.

British Columbia's mountains were not as high as those in Peru. She stared through the windscreen as they took off, and reminded herself of his words. Not so high, and, if she died, if they crashed into the rock, he would be with her and oh, God, even if he could not love her she could not bear it if all she ever had of him was three days!

She squeezed her eyes tight as the world tilted and she prayed, and stayed that way for a long time, begging God to let her have longer. All her life she had thought it was love she'd felt for Alan, but she had not even dreamed that love could feel like this, and maybe, if she had long enough, maybe loving him would do something to Max too and maybe, just maybe, if she was incredibly lucky, he would come to love her. One day he might look at her and she would see it in his face. Not just desire, but the deep tenderness of love and trust.

She had seen his eyes this morning when the dawn had caught them in passion. She knew that, along with the physical desire he felt for her, there was a deep vein of distrust.

She opened her eyes and they were high above the earth. The city was gone, replaced by a patchwork quilt of greens and browns. Springtime in Canada, farmland all colours of fertility. Ahead she could see the mountains, angry rock jutting out from glaciers and snow.

She stared ahead in terrible fascination as Max began to tell her about the formation of these mountains, his voice warm with the eagerness of a man passionately interested in the earth and its secrets. They were communicating through the speakers in their headsets. She turned away from him and heard his voice while she saw white and black and mountains everywhere, and if there was a village or a town there was no way of knowing from above. No sign of life. For all you could see they might be in the Andes, although if it were Peru they would have to be *very* high to have snow. In this small, unpressurised cabin she would be feeling the symptoms of *soroche*—altitude sickness.

Max was saying something about the Ice Age. She made herself ask questions because his calm voice helped. She stole a glance at his hands on the controls and they were steady and certain. This was not the kind of man to have an accident, a crash in the mountains. She looked up into his face and saw his eyes narrow.

'You're not accustomed to small planes?'

'I'll be all right,' she said. You could hardly move around Peru without climbing into a small plane, but she dared not tell him that or he would wonder even more at her nervousness.

He took one hand away from the controls and rested it on her knee. 'It's OK, Faith. I'll keep you safe. Just relax and enjoy the view.'

'Right,' she agreed. The crazy thing was that when she answered his smile the fear was a little less. She dropped her gaze to the hand resting on her knee. He removed it and she closed her eyes on a jab of pain. What would he have thought if she had reached to grasp his hand? If it were dark... If they were in bed she could do it. In the darkness she reached and touched and her instincts were right. But in the daytime she dared not let him see that she needed more than the night's passion.

She would take what she had, make the most of it. She would be happy with what he wanted to give her, learn not to yearn for the rest. In time...

She opened her eyes and stared out at the mountains that were giving way to rolling hills. 'What's that down there?' she made herself ask. She listened carefully to the answer. She would learn. If she had a little time, she would become as good a Canadian ranch wife as any woman could be.

Somehow, the time passed. Eventually she saw the ranch land coming, sloping fields of what must be hay.

'Soon now,' Max's voice murmured on the speaker in her ear. Then a few moments later he pointed. 'That's your cousin's ranch, between those two hills and up the valley until it turns. About six hundred acres.'

How many hectares was six hundred acres? She would work it out later, look up conversions herself instead of showing her ignorance. She turned to look as they flew over and it was not so different from the hacienda in Peru. She knew that Juan's ranch here was for breeding seed stock, not raising beef for food, but the rolling slopes reminded her of the hacienda somehow. Above them were dark green hills, though, not the sparse hills of *ichu* grass that she remembered above the hacienda. Suddenly the fields below came rushing towards her, tilted slightly. Her heart skipped and the old panic welled up and Max's voice seemed to come from far off.

'That's my place. From the curve in the valley here.'

The world straightened and they were flying level again. *Mine*, he had said. Not *ours*. She would have to earn her place in his life.

'What's that hill called?'

He flicked her a glance, his lips pulling up in amusement. 'Shady Mountain. It's really the beginning of the foothills of the Rocky Mountains. I guess by Peruvian standards it's not a mountain at all.'

She smiled back and for a moment she forgot where she was—floating over the world in a small tin machine. 'It's beautiful.' She meant the words and she could tell that she had pleased him. It was frightening how that excited her.

Would he ever come home from a day in the fields and call out her name as he came through the door? Would he ever come home to her, not the house?

Below her, open fields of green stretched from the small mountains to a thin, winding river. She could see a gently sloping abundance of green, the cattle gathered together in close groups. The plane banked and turned slightly with the valley and, for once, when Faith held her breath it was beauty that grabbed her, not fear of the flying machine.

His home was nestled against the mountain. At the top of the mountain there was snow left over from winter, but the valley was rich and green. As the plane circled the homestead buildings, Faith spotted a shady veranda running along one side of a sprawling family home. Max's house. His veranda. She would make it hers too. In the summer she would have dinners on that veranda, Max's friends and hers. They would eat and laugh in the open air, looking down over the rolling green hills to the lazy river.

That veranda would become her favourite place.

The plane swooped down over the river, flying fast and low. The river was not the raging torrent that was the Apurimac near the hacienda, but it was a full, rushing body of water. From higher up, it had seemed a lazy stream.

'Spring run-off,' Max explained, gesturing to the water. He became busy with controls and she heard the sound of the engine change as the grass runway suddenly clarified ahead of the little plane. Then they touched down and were rushing towards a truck parked up ahead, slowing, bumping to a stop twenty metres away from the truck. A man hurried towards the plane.

'Are we expected?' Faith asked. Of course he must have called to announce when he was coming home, but he hadn't mentioned it to her. That omission seemed an omen of how he would regard her in future. The man beside her was almost a stranger. The house on the hill was a stranger's house, not a home where she would entertain on the veranda. Not hers.

Max was climbing out, throwing back words. 'I radioed ahead. That's Hank come to meet us.'

The foreman. He looked the part. He was long and lean, costumed in battered blue jeans and a checked cotton shirt with a denim jacket swinging open. He wore leather boots and a hat tilted to give shade from the low angle of the sun. Faith pushed her hair back and prepared to smile at the foreman. She did not belong, but she would make them accept her.

Max helped Faith out of the plane, then turned to Hank. 'My wife, Faith,' he said abruptly.

It was obvious that the last thing Hank had expected was a wife coming back with his boss. Faith pushed at her hair, a nervous gesture she stilled at once. She made sure her smile was intact and stepped forwards with her hand out. 'Hello, Hank. I've heard a lot about you. I'm so glad to meet you.'

The man recovered quickly, mumbling something about it being great to meet her and choking off what must have been stunned astonishment. She wondered briefly if a handshake was appropriate between a man and woman meeting in Canada. In Peru it was, but here... It must be all right. Hank shook her hand briefly.

Hank began to load the luggage from the plane into the back of the pick-up truck.

'We'll walk up,' Max said.

Hank tossed another bag into the pick-up. 'Not your missus. Not in those shoes.'

Max glanced at her high heels. 'No,' he agreed, and Faith felt like a *thing* they were discussing.

'You can go ahead,' she said. 'I don't mind coming after in the truck.'

Max shook his head. Was he realising how odd it would look to his foreman if he let his wife come to their home alone for the first time?

'Gonna tie her down?' demanded Hank in a husky voice.

Faith suppressed a gasp.

'In a bit,' Max replied. 'No wind right now.'

They *couldn't* be talking about her. Of course couldn't.

Hank made a gesture to the plane. 'If you want me to...'

'No,' said Max, and Hank grinned as if this was an old joke. He turned to Faith and she still had her smile working, although she was the one here who did not understand, who did not belong.

'He never says yes,' Hank explained. 'Never lets anyone touch that plane of his. Doesn't trust us with it.'

The plane! They were talking about tying the airplane down.

In the truck, she sat between the two men, feeling her body sway with the uneven ground they rode over. Once she lurched against Max and for a moment she gave in to temptation and leaned against him before she caught herself and sat erect. He looped an arm around her shoulders and pulled her back to rest against him.

She closed her eyes and let the sensation soak in. His arm around her, herself leaning against his chest. The gesture might be for Hank's benefit, but if she could sit here forever...

'Tired?' he murmured.

'A bit,' she admitted in a husky voice.

'You flew up from that place in Mexico?' asked Hank, glancing sideways at Faith.

'Yes,' she agreed, forcing her eyes to be alert. 'But we've taken two days over the trip.'

'Faith comes from Peru,' Max said just as the truck stopped beside the sprawling ranch house.

They came into the house through the back door, both men burdened by baggage so that Faith opened the door for them. She wondered if she should have carried something. She hadn't thought to offer and now it seemed too late. In Peru a woman would never carry a suitcase, but women here were the equals of men, weren't they? They were partners, and she should have picked up something from the back of the truck.

She closed the door behind the men once they were in. She was in a big utility room set lower than the rest of the house. The door to what had to be a massive kitchen was standing open. There had once been a step up to the kitchen, but someone had built a ramp over the step.

Should she go back out and get one of the remaining bags? Faith hovered, undecided what was expected of her. She had her hand on the doorknob when a woman rolled down the ramp from the kitchen. Sarah, Hank's wife. She was small and blonde, with a cap of short, boyish hair. She was in a wheelchair with big, shiny wheels, and as she halted in front of Max she grinned up at him.

Faith wished she had changed somewhere between Denver and the ranch. She was overdressed, in a silk skirt and blouse, matching raw silk jacket and high heels. Max was more casual, in tailored trousers and a tweed sports jacket. The woman in the wheelchair was wearing jeans and laughing up at Max as he bent to kiss her cheek.

'Been behavin'?' he demanded sharply.

Her laughter bubbled into a husky sound of delight. 'While you were on holiday, I scrambled the computer, used your hot pool every evening, and had wild parties up here. The place is trashed!'

'Can't get good help these days, can I?' Max glowered as he stood up straight, but Faith could see laughter in his eyes. 'I can't leave this place for a minute.'

'Tough!' retorted the woman saucily. 'Take it or leave it.'

'I'll take it,' he drawled.

Something flashed between the woman in the wheelchair and the foreman at Faith's side. Faith felt a wave of envy roll over her. Just that simple look between a man and his wife. No need for words. Hank and Sarah Beston were so secure in each other's love that they only needed a glance to communicate.

Sarah's smile died when she saw Faith. 'Hello? I didn't know Max had brought a guest.' Her smile came back and she spoke with the confidence of a woman who was the natural hostess in this place. She began to wheel her chair towards Faith. 'I'm Sarah,' she announced.

'I'm Faith. I've been looking forward to meeting you.' She thought her words sounded stilted. A guest. Naturally Sarah had assumed Faith was a guest.

'My wife,' said Max.

Sarah's smile faltered.

CHAPTER NINE

IT WAS a noisy party, voices raised and conversation enthusiastic. These people were a community. Gatherings brought out stories and laughter.

Faith wasn't sure where Max was. He'd been talking to his sister the last time she saw him. Then, when Faith looked for him a few moments later, he was gone. She swept the room surreptitiously with her eyes, then smiled again at the rancher who was explaining that a stampede was a rodeo and an exhibition all in one. When he faltered, she asked another question and he was off again, telling her all the details his own wife knew too well.

Faith was learning about ranching fast, memorising details and names. She was working hard to ensure that Max's friends liked her, hiding her headache and smiling. Mostly, the smiles were returned, but Max's sister Beth was another matter. Whenever Faith felt Beth's eyes on her, she smiled at the other woman. Once Beth had smiled back before she'd turned away. A very mechanical smile. Not sincere.

This was Beth's party, an informal wedding reception for her brother and his bride. A welcome-Faith party, but there was no welcome in Beth's eyes. Just suspicion.

Max's ex-fiancée was here. Faith wasn't going to win any popularity contests there either. Alice was on the other side of the room, partnered by a lanky man who frowned whenever he looked at Max. Once, when Faith had looked across the room, she had seen Max deep in conversation with Alice. Max and Alice. Even their names sounded as if they belonged together.

They looked good together too. Alice was tall and lean and beautiful. She had short blonde hair that curled softly. When Max stood near her, they looked like an exercise in colour co-ordination. Faith knew that it was ridiculous for her to feel that she did not belong because of her own exotic appearance, but looking at Alice made her too aware of her own dark curls and pale ivory skin.

And yet Canada was a country peopled by every sort of person, a fact that was obvious in this gathering. The man educating her about rodeos spoke with a thick German accent. His wife had come to Canada from Chile when she was a baby. The woman by the door was the daughter of a native Haida chieftain. Her blond husband was from Alaska. Some of these people, like Max and his sister, had been born in the valley. More had come from other places, sometimes the other side of the world.

'It's a good country for the cattle,' the German-Canadian was telling her.

'Yes,' she agreed, because she knew it was true. It was a wild country, but she was accustomed to that. Peru was wild and often much more primitive than this place.

'A good country for the heart, too,' added the tough old rancher, surprising her with the warm sentiment in his eyes. 'A man can love this place. You'll come to love it in time.'

'I think I already have,' she confessed, and this time her smile was completely genuine, filled with new memories...

Morning, the dawn flowing pink over the fields. She loved the dawn, loved to stand on the veranda drinking a cup of the coffee she had made for Max, staring out over the fields and feeling the country come awake. She had never felt such an intimate connection to the countryside before. Whenever she'd visited the Corsica hacienda in Peru, she had always been served morning coffee in bed. Somehow the hacienda had seemed sedate and controlled by the time she'd risen. In Lima, the city had overwhelmed the nearby mountains. Seattle had also been a city place for Faith, and even in Spain the village had extended far enough to insulate her from the countryside.

The ranch might be Max's alone, but watching the sunrise from the veranda, sharing the dawn with the valley—that was a magic no one could take from her. Sometimes she looked back when she heard Max come into the kitchen and yearned for him to join her to watch the sky change colour. If only he would put his arm around her and share the magic of dawn with her!

He hadn't. Not yet. So when he came into the kitchen, she always hurried inside and put his breakfast in front of him.

'You don't need to do this, Faith,' he'd protested that first morning. 'I'm used to getting my own and I'm always up early. You could sleep in.'

She had smiled at him, and although his lips had not curved his eyes had answered her smile. 'I like to get up early,' she had said, because she could not say that she wanted to do everything for him, to *become* everything to him.

She cooked his breakfasts, learning what he liked and becoming accustomed to the Canadian food on his shelves. The freezer was filled with beef. Coming from a family that raised beef in Peru, that seemed normal enough. But there were no tortillas anywhere, while half the preserves in the pantry seemed unfamiliar to her.

'What do I do about grocery supplies?' she asked him the second morning.

'There's a store in the village.' He was on his way out to do his morning chores, turned back to answer with thinly disguised impatience. 'It's not very well stocked though. Can you drive a truck?'

'No, I can't drive at all.'

'You'll have to learn. I certainly can't be driving you around all the time.' He sighed. 'You'd better ask Sarah if she can drive you into Williams Lake.'

That was when Faith learned that Max had bought a van with special modifications to allow Sarah to drive. No wonder Max felt impatient—his wife needed the help of a woman in a wheelchair to get to town.

'I'll learn,' she said. 'I can learn to drive if you'll teach me.'

'I don't have time for that.' He made an impatient gesture. 'When Beth and Wayne get back, you'd better ask Beth to arrange lessons for you.'

Beth. His sister who lived on the other end of the valley. Beth and her husband were away for a few days with their son. Faith had yet to meet them. She was hoping that Beth would become a friend, but of course it wasn't that easy.

She met Beth that same day. Faith had found the stores of flour and yeast in the pantry. The flour was wonderful and glutinous. As she kneaded it she could feel the elastic strength of it. This would make wonderful yeast rolls. She'd learned to make the rolls at the orphanage and believed that Max would love them. He was a man with a strong appetite and an appreciation of good food.

At night he had a strong appetite, too. Faith shivered with the memory. Would Max's desire for his wife abate with time? Would the touch of loving fade until the nights were like the days? They were strangers by day...lovers at night.

She kneaded and punched and turned the mass of dough on the board. Behind her, she heard heavy footsteps and the slam of a door. She turned, her hands filled with the raw dough. The woman who came through the door was heavy with advanced pregnancy. She stopped in the doorway, the little boy behind her pressing against her leg.

'Who are you?' It was the boy who asked the question.

The woman rested her hand on the curve of her belly. She was slightly breathless, her brown hair short and wavy. Faith started to move towards her, stopped when she realised her hands had dough all over them.

'I'm Faith,' she said breathlessly. 'You must be Max's sister. Do you want to sit down?'

Beth shook her head sharply. 'We just got back last night. I just heard—I didn't believe it.'

Faith forced herself to smile. 'Max and I are married,' she said, and although Beth had obviously already heard that news she still looked stunned.

'But he—Alice—where did you meet my brother?'

'In Mexico.' Faith knew her face was flushing. Beth was staring at her as if she could see that first meeting, Faith rushing down the beach dressed in nothing but a bit of lace and Max strolling out of the water towards her.

'Mexico?' Beth echoed. 'But Max was going to Juan Corsica's island and... How long have you known my brother?'

Faith lifted her head higher. 'Two weeks.'

'But Max wouldn't...' Beth gestured helplessly. 'He wouldn't marry a stranger.'

Faith put all the confidence she could into her smile. 'I'd hardly call Max and me strangers.'

'Are you my aunt?' demanded the boy suddenly. 'You don't look like an aunt.'

'Jerry!' snapped Beth. 'Mind your manners.'

No, she had not got off to a good start with Max's sister. Faith caught sight of Beth moving slowly through the party guests now. She was younger than her brother, probably in her early thirties. She was also in the last stages of her pregnancy and obviously exhausted from the party preparations. Faith had offered to help with the food, but Beth had refused.

Faith didn't think there was any way she could have changed that first meeting with Beth. The other woman was not eager to like her new sister-in-law, although she was certainly going through the motions with this party. If Beth didn't approve of her brother's choice, at least no one else in the district was going to know.

'Max's little wife,' drawled a woman's voice behind Faith.

Alice Donovan. They had been introduced earlier. 'Alice, our librarian,' someone had announced. No one had mentioned that Alice had once planned to marry Faith's husband.

Faith turned around with a smile already on her lips. When she met Alice's eyes she found only resentment there. 'Where did our Max find you?' wondered Alice in a lazy voice, her eyes roving over Faith in a way that made her feel soiled.

'Mexico,' Faith said crisply, forcing her smile to stay in place. 'We met in Mexico.' She shrugged and made her smile soften as if with private memories. Deliberately, she softened her voice as well. 'Max and I... it was love at first sight. Tropical nights...' Her voice trailed off suggestively.

Anger flared into Alice's eyes. 'That's not the way I heard it,' she growled. Then she turned and stormed away through the crowd.

Faith clenched her hands into fists and tried to let her smile fade naturally. If Max meant to resume his relationship with Alice...

Watching Alice's back threading through the people who were Max's friends and neighbours, Faith knew she would do anything in her power to prevent Max going to another woman. He was hers! Wedding-rings had been exchanged. She could not bear it if he... The image made her shudder with pain, fury rising underneath.

It was true that she had forced herself on Max, pressured him into this marriage. But Alice didn't know that, would *never* know unless Max told her.

'Faith?'

She turned to Sarah's voice with relief. Sarah was dressed in a light flowered dress that brought out golden tones in her blonde hair. A matching shawl was draped on the back of her wheelchair seat. She was swinging her chair slightly in a motion that Faith had learned to interpret as restlessness.

'Will you push me outside?' asked Sarah.

Sarah was more than capable of wheeling herself on to the veranda, but Faith was grateful for the chance to get away for a moment.

Outside it was cool, the heat of the daytime sun gone.

'Are you warm enough?' she asked Sarah with concern. Unlike Beth, Sarah's original suspicion had quickly turned to approval of Faith.

'I'm fine.' Sarah took control of the chair herself, swinging it so that she was facing Faith. 'You're the one who's shivering. Not used to our cool evenings?'

'I'll learn,' Faith said grimly.

'Or else?' suggested Sarah gently.

Faith grimaced. 'Do I sound sulky?'

Sarah grinned. 'Determined, let's say.'

She sighed. For the first time since the party had begun, Faith felt she could relax. She rested her hands on the rail and looked out over the shadowed yard. Sarah had become a good friend in only a few days. Oh, she had been suspicious of Faith at first, but when Faith had asked Sarah to drive her to town, the other woman had agreed after only a brief hesitation. On the way to Williams Lake, Faith had confessed she couldn't drive. Sarah had offered to teach her.

Max had been sceptical of Faith learning on the hand controls of Sarah's van. Sarah had laughed. 'Someone on the ranch should learn to drive my van. You're hopeless in it and Faith will learn quickly. She'll find it easy enough to change over to foot controls later.'

It was Sarah who'd explained to her that Max had an account with a big grocery supplier in Williams Lake, Sarah who'd explained the procedure for getting a learner's permit to drive and had taken Faith to the government office where she could get the permit. Sarah was giving Faith all the information she hesitated to ask Max for. Faith was grateful.

A few days ago, when Beth had telephoned to say she'd arranged a wedding reception for Max and Faith, Max had turned from the telephone with a frown. 'Saturday night,' he'd announced. 'Beth's having a party for us at her place.'

'What should I wear?' Faith had begun wearing the jeans and cotton shirts Max had insisted she buy in Denver. But jeans for a party?

Max had shrugged the problem away. 'Wear whatever you want.'

It was Sarah who'd helped her. 'Let's look at what you've got,' she had offered. She'd rolled along the row of suits and dresses in Faith's wardrobe, murmuring, 'Too formal...too elegant for a country party... no...no... Here! Yes, try this one on. It's perfect!'

It was a deceptively casual dress made from a rusty colour of silk. The skirt swirled slightly when Faith walked. She had always liked it. In Peru she might have worn it for afternoon tea in a formal home.

Here it was perfect for an evening party. It made her seem a little taller than she was, but the deceptive simplicity and softness of the lines made her comfortable in the mixed gathering that was Beth's party.

'Did you really need fresh air?' she asked Sarah now, watching the other woman lean her head against the head-rest of her chair.

'I just wanted to give *you* a breather.' Sarah shrugged. 'You could hardly refuse to wheel a handicapped woman out on to the porch, so you're not escaping the crowd in there—just being considerate to your husband's bookkeeper.'

Faith chuckled. 'Sarah, you're a fraud! You're the least handicapped person I've ever met. I'm the one who's handicapped. I can't drive. I can't get ready for a small party without help, haven't a clue what to wear.'

Sarah waved a hand in dismissal. 'The dress is great. Perfect. And you're learning to drive.'

'Thanks to you.' She frowned with worry.

Sarah said softly, 'You look the perfect glowing bride and they all love you.'

'Not Alice.' And not Beth.

'Alice Donovan looks like a scarecrow beside you.'

Faith could see the party through the glass door she'd closed when they'd come out. Her eyes sought and found Max. He was talking to a man whose name she couldn't remember. Tom? Tim? No, Patrick! Yes, that was it. As she watched, Max threw his head back and laughed. She wished she knew what they'd said. She wanted to know all the things that made him laugh.

'Sarah...' She cleared her throat. 'When I was talking to Alice, did it show that I—that I...'

'That you were wildly jealous of her?'

'Then it showed?'

'I doubt anyone else realised. You look so confident. You certainly intimidated Alice.' Sarah chuckled. 'One thing I can tell you for sure: Alice got your message. Not that Max *would* of course, but Alice knows that if she even tries it on with your man you'll scratch her eyes out.'

Once before, she'd sat on the sidelines while her marriage evaporated. This time would be different. She was older, stronger. Max might not love her yet, but he liked her and he certainly desired her. Love might come with time.

'You're crazy about our Max, aren't you?' Sarah's question was soft.

Faith blinked back the sudden moisture in her eyes. 'Yes.' And she would fight to the end of her strength if anything threatened their future together.

'That's what I told Hank.' Sarah wheeled her chair a few feet and then turned to wheel back. 'At first I was worried, of course. I mean, you'd obviously just met, and I was afraid you'd made a set for him because he's a wealthy man. But when I saw the way you looked at him...'

Could Max see the love that seemed obvious to Sarah? Max did not want words of love from her. Or even looks of love, perhaps. Uneasily, she licked her lips. 'How did Max and Alice... What happened?'

Sarah spread her hands expressively. 'Officially, she threw him over.'

'Officially?'

'Why don't you ask Max? I've made my own guesses, but your husband doesn't confide his love life in me.'

Ask Max. It was the last thing she could do.

Through the glass, Faith saw Max turn away. He was looking for someone. After a moment his eyes settled on the door to the veranda and he came towards her. She was certain that he couldn't see out from the lighted room, but she was caught motionless as if trapped by his eyes.

When he opened the door, he saw her. He came two steps on to the veranda and it was Sarah he touched, his hand on her shoulder. Not Faith.

'What are you doing out here in the cold, Sarah?'

'I asked Faith to bring me out so I could get a break from the crowd. There's fresh air out here, and Hank's talking to Sandy McHerson. Why doesn't someone tell Sandy that cigar of his is polluting the air?' Sarah swung her chair towards the door. 'I'll leave you two out here. I'm ready to go back now.'

With a smile for both of them and a lingering look of worry in her eyes, Sarah wheeled through the open door into the house.

'She's incredible,' said Faith softly.

'Yes,' Max agreed. 'She is.' He stared at her.

'Did I spill my soup?' she asked uncomfortably. She could read nothing on his face, but she was learning to sense his emotions. He kept them behind those eyes, hidden, except that sometimes the warmth slipped through, or he suddenly threw back his head and laughed.

It was one of the things she was learning to love about him: strong emotions hidden below the surface, sometimes discernible if she looked.

Laughter floated out through the open door and she turned to watch a group of men that included Hank. 'It must have been a funny joke,' she said. In a moment she would have to go back inside. She would have to put her smile back on so that no one could see her doubts. She had to make them accept her. That was a necessary part of getting Max to trust her.

She had worn a mask at the other wedding reception, too. It had been a bigger party, wealthy Lima welcoming Alan because they were realists and a marriage was a marriage even if they did not approve of the groom. For Faith, disillusion had already set in then. Her smile had been stiff and awkward, a pretence that she knew was expected of her. If her marriage was not ideal, Lima society did not want to know about it, nor did her family.

'What's going on in your mind now?' asked Max suddenly.

She saw his gaze drop to the soft caress of silk over the curve of her bodice. She thought his eyes flared. She heard the soft gasp from her throat, an answer to what she'd seen in his face and saw, a clear image of later, his hands teaching her once again to need him.

'What do you think is on my mind?' she asked huskily.

'Heaven knows.' He frowned and abruptly the intimacy was gone. 'I'm beginning to realise how good you are at putting on an act.'

'An...an act?'

His head jerked towards the party. 'Charming them all. Smiles and soft words and they're all in love with you.'

But you're not. She almost said the words. It hurt, holding them back. Holding back the sudden need for tears. She cried too easily. She had to learn to change that.

'I thought you were a weak thing, Faith. That you needed protection.'

'I'm...not...weak.' It was hard getting the words out, difficult to talk at all. She watched him curl his hand around the rail of the veranda and she stared at his long fingers, hating the fact that even when she could feel his resentment of her she could not look at his fingers without remembering the breathless madness of their loving. She could see the anger growing in him, as if standing at her side was unbearable for him.

'No,' he agreed. 'You're not weak. You're a hard woman who knows exactly what she wants and plans to get it.'

She lifted her chin. It was him she wanted. His love. He was staring at her and she stared back. Was there any chance that she could win love from him?

'You're talking about our marriage?'

'Of course I'm talking about our marriage. He crammed his hands into his pockets. No moon tonight. No hint of romance unless you counted the smell of the fresh fields and evergreens on the slopes. And, a hand's reach away, Max with the scent of anger carried close. 'I saw you back there in that room. All those people, and you were looking for someone special in the crowd.'

She had been looking for him. For her love.

'Were you thinking of Alan tonight?'

She swallowed and tilted her head back. 'A little while ago,' she admitted. 'I was thinking of the reception we had when we first went to Peru after our elopement.'

'Damn you,' he growled.

'Max——'

He laughed harshly. 'Don't say any more. You've said enough.'

She gasped. 'What do you mean?'

'I mean that I'm finished playing Alan's part for you.' There was something terrible in his stance. More than anger. Then he turned so she could not see his face. 'I'm not going to be a substitute for another man,' he said harshly. 'I want a wife in my bed, not an actress. Oh, you're a very skilled actress, I admit, but I'm tired of the game. I want the real thing.'

Deliberately, he turned and looked back into the room. Two people moved apart, and through the gap between them Faith could see the tall, willowy form of Alice Donovan.

'The real thing,' he repeated softly.

She felt nausea welling up. 'Are you saying... are you saying you... you want a—a divorce?'

He turned back to her and shrugged. 'It's not necessary, is it? I like your cooking, and you wanted a child. Well——' he shifted his shoulders again '—it's possible you're pregnant. If not, maybe we'll try again some time.'

She felt the pain, but it was like a thing apart from her. Part of her recognised the need to scream at him, to cry, to beg him. An actress. An act. Tired of the game. She was only a toy to him. She turned away and she wanted to run, to stumble down the stairs to the lawn, to escape anywhere before the sobs came. In a minute they would come.

If she went down those stairs she might fall, and if she fell he would come to help her, to catch her. If he touched her now, she might scream. She clenched her hands together and took a deep breath and the pain started then, but she could talk.

'If I'm pregnant—no, you're right. There's no reason for us to share a bed again.'

'No reason at all,' he agreed.

She turned to face him and he was bigger than she thought, frightening, with something near hatred on his face. She held her head very high and met his eyes and one day he would remember how it had been. Max might not love her, but what happened to him in her arms was every bit as shattering to him as it was to her. He might want to forget it. He might dislike her. He might even hate her. But he would remember.

'I'd like my own room,' she said tonelessly.

'No. I'll move.'

They stood like that, staring at each other for what seemed an endless time. She wanted to turn away, to hide from him. She could not. For some reason it seemed important to hold his gaze.

Someone came to the door and blocked the light from inside. It was Beth, standing in the doorway, her hand on her belly. Slowly she came out on to the veranda.

'Max?'

Slowly his gaze shifted from Faith's face, swung towards his sister.

Beth had her arms cradled around her pregnancy. 'Wayne drove Bert over to the pass.' Her voice was confused. 'Bert had a flat tyre and Wayne—he's gone.'

Max shook his head as if to clear it. 'I saw him leaving. He should be back soon.'

Beth bit her lip and put her hand on her brother's arm. 'But... it's time.'

'Time?' he echoed.

Faith stepped forward. 'The baby, Max. She's in labour.'

Beth gasped slightly and closed her eyes. Faith moved to her side. 'How far apart are the pains, Beth?'

Beth shuddered and whispered. 'Five. It started suddenly and——'

'Where's the doctor?' demanded Faith.

Max answered. 'Williams Lake.' He moved then. 'I'll call him and then I'll drive you in, Beth.'

When the contraction passed, Beth pulled away from Faith. 'Sorry,' she muttered. They were alone on the veranda now, Max inside telephoning. Beth was back to normal with the contraction gone, obviously uncomfortable that she'd been leaning against the sister-in-law she disapproved of.

'Will you be going to the hospital to have the baby?'

'Yes, of course.'

In the village in Spain, the women had delivered their babies at home. 'Do you have a bag ready? I could get it for you. Or would you prefer to get it yourself?'

'I don't want them to see me like... this. Oh...' Beth closed her eyes and gasped, and if this was another contraction Faith was certain it was far less than five minutes.

'Let me help you out to Max's truck, then.'

Beth shook her head, her eyes closed.

Faith saw the moment when the spasm eased. 'Look, I know you don't like me, but you're a woman about to have a baby and I do know a bit about that. You could do worse than let me help you.'

Beth stared at her. 'You've never had a baby.'

'No, but I've been staying with my cousin in Spain. Her husband's a doctor and I helped him several times with deliveries. Believe me, Beth, I may be a foreigner, but having babies is the same in any language.'

Beth shook her head confusion. 'I don't exactly dislike you. I just...'

'Max's your brother,' said Faith. 'I understand.'

Beth's eyes closed briefly and her hand stiffened on her belly. 'I want him to have—he deserves...'

This contraction was short and not as severe as the last. Faith wished she knew what that meant. 'Can I help you to Max's truck?' she asked when it was over.

'I'd never make it up into the truck. My station wagon.'

'Where is it?'

'Over there.'

'The keys?'

'In it. I—I feel strange. Almost as if...' They started moving together towards the stairs. 'You'll never forgive me if I get sick all over that gorgeous dress of yours.'

'Yes, I will.' Faith gave the other woman's shoulder a reassuring squeeze. 'Can you do these stairs?'

She could, and they got down to the drive.

'Can you really do babies?' Beth worried. 'If junior's in a hurry, we might not make it to the hospital.'

'We'll manage.'

Beth let out a jagged breath. 'It's crazy. I mean, I've done this before, but it still scares me a bit.'

Faith swallowed a lump of emotion. 'Think of the end,' she said. 'Think of the baby. It's worth it.'

Beth smiled. 'Oh, yes. You know, I—I could have been nicer to you. I just...'

'I do understand. It's all right.' Faith opened the door to the station wagon and Beth sat down awkwardly in the back seat of the car.

'Thanks, Faith.'

Faith said softly, 'I do love your brother, you know, Beth.'

In that instant, a strong contraction gripped Beth.

Someone grasped Faith's arm from behind. 'Get into the house!' snapped Max. 'Someone has to stay and look after Jerry.'

'No!' Beth wailed from the car. 'Max...Faith—I need her with me!'

Faith stood erect, pulling her arm free of his grip. 'I'm going with her in the car. She wants me.'

'What use would you be?' he growled.

'I've helped Antoine deliver babies.'

'And she wants you with her. Of course she does.' His voice was ironic. 'You've charmed *her*, too. Telling her you love me in that soft, persuasive voice.' He laughed again and Faith choked on the harshness in his voice. '"I do love your brother..." No wonder she believed you when you used that voice...the same voice you use on me when we're in bed. Did you tell her why you married me?'

She could not have answered a word. It was hatred in his voice.

'Always lies, isn't it, my darling wife?' His hand gripped her arm again, the fingers cruel and angry. 'God, you're an incredible actress! I've been watching you all evening with my friends and you're a pro. That smile didn't slip once.'

She was a good actress, years of practice at boring parties. But what she had told his sister was the truth. God help her, but she would love this man forever, whether he wanted her or not.

CHAPTER TEN

THE telephone rang just before noon on Thursday. Faith was in the kitchen putting the finishing touches to Max's lunch. Sarah had given her a recipe for soup that she swore Max loved.

She reached for the telephone on the wall when it rang, her eyes still on the table. She knew it was too much to hope that a good meal would make Max smile at her again, but she had added a fresh salad on the side and a tempting dessert.

'Shady Mountain Ranch,' she said automatically, reaching for pen and paper because Max was expecting a call from the lab with the results from some blood samples he had taken from the cattle.

'Faith?'

'Cathy?'

'What in heaven's name are you up to?' Cathy's voice sounded harried.

'Cooking lunch,' she replied automatically. She heard Cathy's gasp.

'That must be a change for you.'

Faith frowned at the annoyance in Cathy's voice. 'Beth just had her baby,' she announced, changing the subject although she knew this call had a purpose. 'A gorgeous baby girl. They're calling her Wendy.' Faith closed her eyes to the memory of that hour with Max in the hospital waiting-room. He'd read a magazine, or at least had turned the pages fairly regularly. Not a word between them, just the echo of his accusations. It had been a relief when Wayne had arrived. They'd both talked to Beth's husband. Not to each other.

'Tell Beth I'm...' Cathy broke off. 'Faith, don't evade the issue. What in God's name have you done?'

Her fingers clenched on the receiver. 'I sent you a wire.'

'You sent it to San Francisco. We were in Brazil. And how on earth——?'

'I didn't expect a hassle from *you*.' She had to get better control of herself. A note of criticism in someone's voice and she was fighting off tears. She cleared her throat. 'You were the one who insisted I go to the island.'

A gasp came over the wire. 'Well, I didn't mean you to *marry* a perfect stranger. And Max should have been immune. The whole idea of the trip to the island was for him to get away from all the sympathetic women in the district. Not that he needed help. For a heartbroken man, he was remarkably intact.'

'Cathy, it's all right. I'm fine.'

Cathy cleared her throat. Now it was coming. 'You couldn't have known him more than a few days.'

'A week.' She closed her eyes. 'Is this the lecture from Juan too, or do I get a special one from you?'

'Jack's furious.' Cathy sounded angry too. 'How could Max take advantage of you——?'

'I asked him to marry me. You knew he was there when you sent me out there.'

'My God! I wouldn't... He's a friend of ours, but I wouldn't throw you out on your own with a strange man! I understood he was going to go down there in January. Jack said any time, but it seems it took him until April to get away from his ranch... He was too busy working to be heartbroken about Alice Donovan. Of course I didn't send you there to meet him. Face it, a Canadian rancher isn't going to be able to comprehend a sheltered creature like you!'

'No,' Faith whispered. Was that their problem? Max thought he understood her; he thought she was a liar, a world-class actress, even when they were in bed together.

'Cathy, I thought you of all people would understand.' She should have known Cathy would not dump her alone on an island with a man. Cathy was reckless sometimes, but not crazy. Even Cathy knew you didn't marry a man you'd known only a week. A man who didn't love you.

'You're in love with him,' Cathy breathed. 'What about him? Is he in love with you?'

'Cathy, please don't...'

'You can't marry a man who doesn't love you.' It wasn't the first time Cathy had said that to Faith.

Something warned her. Some sound. She turned and he was there, standing in the doorway. Home for lunch and glowering at her. What had he heard her say to Cathy?

'Cathy? Listen, I've got to hang up.'

Cathy's irritation shifted to warm concern. 'Are you all right?'

Nothing was right. Not with that look in Max's eyes. Staring back at him, she knew that nothing would ever be right again.

'Faith——'

'Later. I'll call you later.' She had a vision of Juan walking into this ranch house to straighten out her problems. 'Don't—don't tell Juan.' That was crazy. Cathy told Juan everything.

'Don't tell him what?'

That Max did not love her. She swallowed and replaced the receiver.

Max said nothing. His eyes bored into hers.

'Lunch is ready.' She took a bowl with shaking hands and moved to the soup pot.

'That was Cathy Corsica on the telephone?'

'Yes.' Miraculously, she ladled the soup into the bowl without spilling a drop. She carefully placed the steaming bowl on the table.

'It was all planned, then?' Max was still standing, staring at Faith and ignoring the soup. 'You? Me? The island? A good prospect for you because you needed a husband to get a baby—but you preferred not to have a Latin man. So you and Cathy cooked up this little scheme.'

'No! It wasn't like that!'

'Tell me, then, my lovely wife.' It was not a smile that curved his lips. 'How was it?'

She swallowed and swallowed again, her hands rubbing the denim of her jeans. 'I—I—you—I liked you and...' Loved him. Would always love him. His eyes told her he'd never believe the words. He laughed. She shuddered at the sound.

He prowled across the kitchen like a predator stalking prey.

She backed up against the counter, her hands spread out behind her.

'Liked me? What sort of *like*, Faith? You thought of yourself as a commodity, didn't you? Woman on the marriage market. Services in exchange for room and board and a baby.' He stopped and there were only inches of tension between her trembling body and his anger.

'You sold yourself.' He shrugged angrily. 'Hell, why not? You were ready to sell yourself to Jorge. You sold yourself to me instead, but what exactly did you gain? The chance to have a baby, and a kitchen. Jorge would have given you a baby, but no kitchen. Was it worth it?'

She sucked in a shaken breath. In a way, it *had* been like that. Her own family had treated her as a commodity, her uncles pushing Jorge at her. But she had met Max and, the first time he touched her, going to Jorge had become impossible. Even then, back on the island, she'd known this was a man she could not walk away from.

She had not dreamed that, in pressuring Max to marry her, she had destroyed any chance she might have had to win love from him. She reached her hand out, a plea, but when she touched his chest he jerked away and she gasped with the pain of his rejection.

'What is it you want me to be?' she whispered.

'A telling question.' She saw the muscles in his throat clench. 'If I tell you what I want, will you deliver?'

She wrapped her arms around her waist. 'I'll try,' she whispered unsteadily.

'My God! I vowed I'd never be the kind of fool my father was, but I've fallen into a very different trap, haven't I? Every man's dream. The woman who will give whatever he asks, play any role.' His voice rose to accusation. 'How do you get yourself in the mood when bedtime comes, Faith? Memories of Alan?' He leaned forward and grasped her chin to force her head up. 'Look at me, damn you!'

She blinked to fight the tears.

'If you cry, so help me, I'll throttle you!'

'What happened between your father and mother?'

He pulled his hand away from her. She wanted to reach for him, to touch, to use the one power she seemed to have over this man—his own passion. But not now. With hate in his eyes, her touch would not turn his distance to love, not even the physical echo of love.

'Why?' he demanded. 'What the hell have my parents to do with this?'

A lot, she thought. 'I'd...I'd like to know about your mother.' He'd talked of his father, the man who had been a stern friend to Max and Beth, who had died when Max was in his mid-twenties, practising veterinary medicine in nearby Williams Lake. His father's death had brought Max back to the ranch he'd grown up on, but the ranch had been almost bankrupt. Max had worked hard to turn it into the successful enterprise it now was. She had learned a little of his past from him, more from Sarah. But the only thing she'd ever heard about his mother was that she lived in Vancouver.

He was prowling restlessly. 'Do you think knowing will help you play your part?'

'I've never played a part with you.'

The sound from his throat wasn't laughter. 'For God's sake, Faith! Stop the lies! You're welcome to the information. My mother's a very young sixty-year-old lady living in Vancouver. If this fiasco of a marriage lasts, which I doubt it will, you'll meet her one day. Not here. She wouldn't come within a hundred miles of this place. My father was mad about her. When she demanded he sell the ranch and head for the city, he'd have done that for her. Except that times were bad then and he was too heavily mortgaged. He'd have gone bankrupt if he sold out—and my darling mother isn't one for suffering. So she left us.'

'Left her children? Oh, Max...'

He jerked away from her touch.

'How old were you?' Would he ever let her touch him again?

'Old enough.' He turned to glare at the steaming soup on the table. 'I'm not hungry. From now on, pack me a lunch in the morning.'

After that, she hardly saw him. He got up in the morning, drank the coffee she made and picked up his Thermos and the lunch she made. He never returned before dark. The first time he found her waiting in the kitchen with his supper, he said tonelessly, 'Next time I'm late, just leave me a plate to microwave.' He did not want her waiting up for him.

When he was home, he was either shut in his office or sleeping in the bedroom down the hall. She hadn't realised how much they had talked, how much it meant to her, until he withdrew from her. They'd chatted about their plans for the day over breakfast, sharing news over lunch and supper. There'd been no words of love, but there had been companionship, and it was gone now.

And the nights...

She slept poorly, her eyes aching from the tears she could not shed in the day. The days went by and she began to fear that he would never come to her. Given time, she had told herself, he would want her again. When he did, in the deep sharing of their bodies she would be able to tell him how much she loved him. Would he believe her?

He did not love her, but she knew now that she was endangering their future by hiding her own love. If she had realised that sooner, she might have found the courage to tell him. If only she had known he'd had a selfish mother who'd abandoned him because her husband would not give her the luxuries and the city life she wanted. A selfish woman who had destroyed her son's trust.

A commodity, Max had called Faith, and she could see how he believed that. She had been returning to Peru to do what her family wanted. Compromising, because she'd come to believe she'd never find love. If she'd married Jorge her family would have been happy and she could have had a child. It wasn't an unusual compromise for a woman to make in Peru, but after only two weeks in Canada she could see how foreign it was. If she'd been a Canadian woman, she would have gone out and found a job, or wrested control of Alan's factory from her uncles and managed it herself.

Impossible in Peru.

I love you.

Would he believe her if she said the words?

On Monday, Cathy called again to tell Faith that she and Juan would be arriving on Wednesday. 'We'd like you and Max to come to dinner Wednesday night.'

'All right,' said Faith. The inquisition. Juan wanted to be satisfied that all was well. After all, he was a Peruvian man responsible for the well-being of his female relatives.

'Don't worry,' said Cathy, sensing Faith's distress. 'Jack just wants you to be happy. After compromising to marry a wild American like me, he's not about to pretend he doesn't understand about falling in love. And Max is a friend of his.'

Faith left a note for Max about the dinner invitation. She propped it on the table where he would sit to eat his reheated dinner tonight. He would not be home for lunch. Never again. Wednesday. Only two days away. Juan wanted the best for Faith. If he talked to Max...

The way things were now, Max might tell Juan their marriage was a failure. Once he'd told her they were going to make this marriage work. Now... he'd be more than happy for Juan to take Faith back to Peru.

A commodity. Unsatisfactory merchandise.

She'd never see him again.

He would never send her away if she were expecting his child. He would never abandon his own child. Faith crossed her arms over her abdomen. Max didn't know that her period had come last week, but if he asked her she would have to tell the truth. There was no child. He was free to send her away.

If only she could have a little more time.

He'd asked her not to stay up to serve his dinner. But if she was going to be a Canadian woman she should practise a little rebellion. She could stay up regardless. She would find every opportunity to remind him that, even if he did not love her the way she loved him, he had once enjoyed sitting with her, talking. She would remind him of how they'd laughed together the time the cat had spent three hours crouched at a gopher hole waiting for the creature to come out.

Max had been learning to care about her. If only he had trusted her a little more. If she had time, a little more time, perhaps...

The telephone rang again.

This time it was Beth, just back from hospital two days before. Her voice was bright and happy. 'This is crazy, but Wayne and I promised Jerry a trip to the river today, and I don't want to disappoint him... The baby wasn't due yet when we promised, and I thought...well, I don't want to make Jerry feel the baby's pushing him out. But it's windy and I don't want Wendy to catch cold.'

'Do you want me to look after the baby?'

Beth jumped at that. 'I was hoping you would. My neighbour offered, but I'd feel better if she was with you.'

She knew that it would hurt, holding Beth's baby, knowing she would never have Max's child growing inside her, in her arms.

Beth and Wayne and Jerry came half an hour later. Beth transferred the baby tenderly into Faith's arms while Wayne carried in a collapsible play-pen that could be used as a cot. Jerry plunked down a bag on the counter.

'Baby's diapers, Aunt Faith,' he announced. 'An' there's a bottle here, too.'

'I'll miss one feeding,' Beth confided uneasily. 'It's formula in the bottle, but it should be OK. She was having formula in the hospital for her night feeding.'

Faith held the tiny bundle in her own arms and assured Beth that they'd get on fine together. Bittersweet.

Wendy was fussing as the truck drove away, squirming in Faith's arms. She went to the rocking-chair and sat with the baby soft and cuddly against her. She'd always enjoyed babies, had always yearned for one of her own. She closed her eyes and told herself that if she could not have her own child she would at least have nieces and nephews.

What would she do if Max sent her away?

Wendy's tiny fist was shoved against her mouth, her eyes closed and her breathing soft. Carefully Faith stood up and carried her into the bedroom where Wayne had set up the play-pen with a soft quilt in it. The pen was against the wall at the foot of the big double bed Faith had shared with Max for such a breathlessly brief time.

Wendy grunted once when Faith put her down, then she shifted her little rear end and found her fist with her mouth. Nothing like a baby sleeping, thought Faith tenderly.

She heard the door open at the other end of the house. It must be Max, although she'd no idea why he would come home in the middle of the day. She curled her hands around the rail of the play-pen and reached for courage. If he stayed more than a moment, she would go to him. She would sit down across from him and somehow make him acknowledge her presence.

He would have come in the kitchen door. He never came in the front door when he was dressed in work clothes. His footsteps echoed across the kitchen floor, then stillness. Faith took a deep breath and released the play-pen.

Max's footsteps came closer. Stopped.

'Faith...?'

She turned, the play-pen behind her. He was there in the doorway, staring at the baby in the pen. For once, his face was not hard, but tender, with his gaze on the baby.

'It's Wendy,' she said breathlessly.

Max had called for her. She had dreamed that he would come home and call out her name. And he had, just now.

'Beth and Wayne promised Jerry an outing,' she explained, speaking softly in case the baby woke. 'But Beth didn't want to risk the baby catching cold.'

'I didn't think she'd trust anyone with Wendy so soon. When she had Jerry...' He looked up and Faith stopped breathing.

'She trusts me.' She bit her lip. 'I wish you would trust me, too.'

'I saw your note.' The softness left his face. 'Juan and Cathy are coming on Wednesday?'

'Yes.'

He took a deep breath, his eyes on her. 'This isn't going to work.'

'Couldn't we try it a little longer?' she whispered, knowing the answer. No good. Too late to repair the damage. He was going to send her away, entrust her to Juan as if she were the commodity he had accused her of being. She caught her bottom lip between her teeth and vowed she would *not* cry.

His eyes were wide, deep with something she could not decipher. With his gaze locked to hers, he slowly walked around the end of the bed towards her.

'What are you going to do?' she breathed.

He stopped in front of her. She stared up at him. She was in stockinged feet, making him seem very tall in his jeans and soft cotton shirt. He had taken his hat off, must have left it in the kitchen. Slowly he bracketed her shoulders with his hand. She felt her body tremble.

'I'm going to use that bed.' His voice was husky.

'The baby...'

'...is asleep. Any other objection?'

'No,' she whispered, although it was not love or even passion she saw in his eyes. It was the end.

He did not kiss her or touch her in any way designed to lure her into passion. Instead he picked her up and carried her out of the room where the baby was sleeping, down the corridor to the guest room.

He did not look down at her once on that long journey down the corridor. He kicked the door closed behind him and she felt fear as he laid her on the bed. She looked for something in his eyes, for some sign of vulnerability, of softness. He stood beside the bed, staring at her as he began to unbuckle his belt.

'Would you... force me?'

His gaze slid down along her body, found the swelling of her breasts under her cotton shirt, the thrust of her denim-clad hips.

Love me, her heart pleaded. Please love me!

He pulled his zip down. 'I can't imagine force being necessary,' he said in a low voice. He stepped out of his jeans. 'You'll play your part. You're very good at it.' His head went up so that he was looking at her through narrowed eyes. 'Take off your clothes,' he ordered.

There was no love in him now, nothing but anger too tightly leashed.

'You heard me, Faith.

Darkness, she thought wildly. In darkness he might let her touch his heart. If only he would touch her with desire and tenderness. Then she would somehow make him understand how deeply she loved him, how she needed his love in return.

Not like this, light blazing through the window and anger in the man.

'Would you... Max... ?'

'No?' he asked softly. 'Don't tell me you're refusing me? My obedient wife.'

She swallowed a cry of protest. 'Would you close the drapes first?' she pleaded in a whisper.

He crossed the room to the window. For a second there were shadows as he closed the heavy curtains, then brilliant light as he switched on the overhead light. He unbuttoned his shirt with one hand as he walked towards her. Then there was nothing covering him but his brief jockey shorts.

'What is it you want?' she whispered.

He did not even pretend a smile. 'I want you to undress. Take off your clothes.'

Her hand fumbled with her buttons. She squeezed her eyes closed because she could not bear that look in his eyes. She had to keep the tears away. Had to... She unfastened the first button of her blouse. The second.

Silence. He was waiting.

It was hopeless. Not love. Just taking, victory, because he hated her now. If he took her body now it would be the end, the final destruction of whatever tenderness he had felt for her.

Her eyes were still closed when his hand came to her breast. His touch was deliberately arousing through her clothing. Her body remembered. Responded. She bit her lip as his hand flattened against her heartbeat. When his thumb rubbed across the peak of her breast she heard the sound torn from her own throat.

'Open your eyes,' he commanded.

She stared up into his face. Harsh. Frightening.

'Say my name.' His hand moved down over her body in an intimate caress. She cried out and her body moved against him, desire flaring as her eyes drifted closed. She could not stop her body's response... could not bear to see his indifference as she lost control.

She reached to touch him.

He caught her wrist. 'Oh, no! Not this time. Look at me!'

She shuddered. 'Turn out the light. Please, Max!'

He leaned over her. 'This time in daylight. You'll watch me. I promise you, this time you'll have no doubt who the man in bed with you is.' He cupped her breast with his hand and stroked the nipple until her eyes glazed with the writhing need in her body.

'Look at me!'

He hated her, staring down into her eyes as he caressed her, moving his hand from her breast, pushing the fabric up and roughly opening the zip to her jeans. He stripped away every scrap of her clothing, then he touched her in the most intimate way and he did not need her broken cry to know that her body ached with passion.

'Say my name,' he demanded, his hand on her and her blood throbbing, her lungs tearing with each breath.

'Max,' she whispered. 'Max, please...! Please don't do this!' She lifted her arm to hide her tears, but the sob grew in her throat and there was nothing she could do to conceal herself from him.

He jerked away from her as if she had burned him. 'How can I be such a damned fool as to want you?'

'Max—I...' It was hardly more than a whisper. 'I love you.'

'Sure you do, baby.' He laughed harshly. 'So long as I don't remind you that it's not Alan in bed with you. So long as I give you the baby you can pretend is your dead husband's.'

She sat up, her breasts heaving with the pain in her eyes. 'I've never thought of Alan when we were together. *Never!*'

'Spare me the hysterics.' He picked up his jeans, left his shirt where it lay on the floor. At the door he stopped. 'Is there any possibility that you're pregnant?'

She shuddered. 'No,' she confessed miserably.

'Then we'll end this fiasco.' He made a gesture of finality. 'I'll give you back to your family. I imagine you can get an annulment. Juan will probably arrange it.'

She was shivering, naked, but his eyes on her were indifferent.

She stared at him, pleading, and knowing there were no words to change the resentment in his eyes. 'An annulment would mean that we'd never...that we...never made love.'

'What difference does it make, Faith? One more lie. And you could hardly call it "love". Go back and make your deal with your tame Peruvian. I'm sure he'll be happy to take Alan's place in your bed.'

'Max, I never thought it was Alan making love to me when I was with you—*nunca!* Never! I never wanted... No one ever made me feel the way you do! I never wanted...'

He was gone, his footsteps echoing in the corridor.

'I love you,' she whispered, but he was gone.

He would not have believed her even if he had heard.

CHAPTER ELEVEN

MAX had just finished letting the calf loose into the field when he saw Faith. She was walking down the short road towards him.

Behind him, Hank grunted, 'She's all right, your lady.' Coming from Hank, it was high praise.

Max sighed and turned back to the corral.

'It's none o' my business,' muttered Hank, 'but you're bein' pretty hard on your lady these days.'

'Yeah,' he admitted. 'I guess I am.'

Hank's mouth opened again, then snapped shut when Max shook his head. 'Don't, Hank. I'm in no mood for advice.'

'Right,' agreed the foreman. 'I'll go sort out those yearlings in the south pasture, should I?'

'Do that. I'll be along in a bit.'

When Hank was gone, Max gave in to the temptation to climb the fence and watch Faith as she came down the hill. Even dressed in blue jeans and an oversized sweater she looked exotic. It was her hair, he supposed, that generous abundance of curly black. And her walk, the way his eyes caught the swing of her hips as she turned the corner at the office. Watching her walk always made him remember the feel of her, the inflaming scent of her flesh in his nostrils...loving her.

She was heading for the office where Sarah was working. Not coming here at all. Max watched her walk away from him, watched until she disappeared inside the office. There had been no reason at all for him to think she was coming to see him.

They'd made a bloody mess of things.

He turned away and stared at the cattle grazing in the next field. A few of them were scattered close enough for him to identify. He catalogued them automatically, his mind on Faith. Soon she would be gone and he would be left alone with his cattle and an empty house. Once he might have managed to tell himself it would be enough, but he had learned to dream these last weeks. He'd imagined her here when winter came. He'd light a fire for her in the big living-room. He'd spend evenings with Faith sitting in the rocking-chair, her arms holding their child. When the child was asleep, he would take the baby from her, lay it gently in the cradle. Then he'd come to his woman, his eyes on her and hers answering and she would whisper his name and they would love.

She was the kind of woman who would stay the winters, who would never cry for the far-away city. They'd travel, of course, but the valley below Shady Mountain would always be home and she would be as eager to return as he was. She'd made a home for herself here, had bonded with everyone from his prickly sister to his sceptical foreman.

Max turned to stare up at the house. When she was gone...

Behind him, a cow bawled. Bessie.

'I don't believe you can tell one from the other,' Faith had teased him once. Her eyes had been all laughter and he had wanted to reach for her and tell her what he felt.

What if he had?

Bessie stared at him with bovine indifference. He glared back.

Then he heard the sound of the jet.

He did not look, but he heard the roar come closer, then the distortion of sound as the flying thing turned to circle. Max knew that sound. He had heard it many times since Juan bought the property west of his.

Juan and Cathy had arrived.

A few hours left. They'd been invited to dinner tonight, although Max might go over earlier and talk to Juan. The Peruvian was going to be very angry. Max might lose a friend as well as a wife today.

Bessie bawled again and her calf moved towards her. Max remembered flying Faith home. She'd asked if the cattle had names and he'd told her about Bessie.

It had been a long night, fighting for Bessie's life in surgery after she'd got through the fence and run in front of a speeding truck. He'd called in a veterinary nurse from Williams Lake to help. The nurse had kept telling him that there was no point, that it was too late. Anyone could see Bessie wasn't going to make it. But Max had fought on through the night.

When dawn had come, he'd won.

Max felt the hairs rising on the back of his neck. He turned slowly. Faith was there, standing on the walk outside the office.

He never needed sight or sound to feel her presence. When she was gone, he would know her absence with every breath he took. Even up on the north slopes he would drown in emptiness.

He gave one look back at Bessie. She stared at him, reminding him that he'd fought hard for the life of a cow.

He wasn't done fighting. Not yet.

Faith came down from the house in the hope of catching sight of Max. Then, when she saw him watching her from the paddock, she lost her courage and turned to go into the office.

Sarah was sitting in her wheelchair at the desk, punching computer keys noisily.

'Stupid bureaucrats!' she was muttering. 'If they want to design a form, they could at least ask for information that's *possible* to give!' She looked up and saw Faith. 'Hi! Don't mind me. It's the bloody Goods and Services Tax report, and I spend my life on this thing every month!'

Faith leaned back against the door.

Sarah pushed her keyboard aside. 'What's wrong?'

If she talked, Faith was afraid she would cry. It was Wednesday and it wasn't a matter of courage. Max didn't want to hear her say she loved him. He would not believe a word she said.

Sarah turned her wheelchair to come around the desk.

'Sarah...' Her voice was strangled. 'If I leave——'

'You're not leaving?' Sarah jerked her chair around a pile of files on the floor.

'If... will Max marry Alice in the end?' Faith didn't want him to be alone forever. She *didn't!* But the image of him with another woman was like a knife in her. Beyond bearing.

'You're not leaving?'

Faith couldn't answer.

'He doesn't love Alice,' Sarah said angrily.

'He doesn't love me either,' said Faith in a voice that shook.

Cathy and Juan would arrive soon. Then dinner, and how exactly would the scene go when Max handed her over to Juan? Forever. It would be forever. Nothing could make it possible for her to pretend to any kind of calmness when the man she loved was pushing her out of his life.

'Well, you *can't* be jealous of Alice!' Sarah said forcefully. 'When Max looks at you, sparks fly. But

Alice—I think he decided it was time to get married and she was there. But then... Well, he wasn't the only man she had on a string. He let her put it around that she was the one breaking it off, but I overheard him telling her and that's not how it was.' Sarah gestured expressively. 'He caught her out. I heard him tell her he wasn't going to marry a woman who was playing a part to get her hands on one of the wealthiest men in the area. She could tell her friends whatever lie she chose, but there wasn't going to be a wedding.'

Playing a part. No wonder Max wasn't willing to listen to her. He'd almost married one woman who was pretending to love him. He must hate Faith and it was a good thing there had not been a child. He would have kept the marriage intact for the sake of his child, but there would never be love.

She heard the roar of the jet then. It might be any jet, but she knew it was Juan. Her family had come to make certain she was all right. Well, she wasn't. She would never be right again. She turned and Sarah was saying something, but Faith could not answer.

She got out to the path and there it was, the jet just turning to head towards Juan's ranch. If Faith had any sense she'd go now, leave and avoid the hours ahead, waiting for tonight. Would Max drive her and her bags to Juan's ranch in the pick-up? Could she bear to sit silently at his side, or would she beg him to let her stay?

Once she would have believed she was too proud to beg any man for love. She had been too proud to say a word to Alan when she'd found he'd been unfaithful to her. But now—if it would help—she would beg Max.

He was still in the paddock. She saw him turn when the sound overhead was gone. Max stared towards her for a long time. She began to move, to walk towards him.

He came out of the paddock and turned away from her, towards the truck parked against the fence.

He started it with an angry growl of the engine. The gearbox complained loudly when he shoved it into reverse. Max was normally a smooth, calm driver. Not now. The truck jerked back, then surged forwards so that Faith jumped. The big tyres braked in a spurt of gravel beside her. He pushed the passenger door open.

'Get in!' he commanded.

She grasped the door with one hand and climbed in. When she pulled he door shut, the truck lurched into motion and she protested, 'My seatbelt's not done up.'

Max was a fanatic about seatbelts, but this time he just glanced at her and she reached for the belt, her hands shaking so badly that she could not get it fastened. He shifted gears and turned away from the house.

'Where are you taking me?'

He shifted again and they were racing along the gravel. In a minute they'd be on the highway and he would turn towards Juan's ranch.

He was getting rid of her now, not waiting for evening.

'Max, I——'

'Don't say a word!'

She hugged herself and stared through the windscreen. Beside the truck, three cows on the other side of the fence scattered away from the noise of the engine. Overhead, an eagle circled lazily, gliding on the wind currents.

The highway was just ahead, and although she had not been to Juan's ranch yet, Max had showed her where it was—five minutes' drive along the paved road.

She would never see Max again.

She was thrown against him as the truck suddenly took a corner on to a small, dirt road that led upwards. She felt the warmth of his shoulder under hers in the instant before she pushed herself away.

'Do up your seatbelt!'

She bit back a retort. She'd never argued with him, never fought back when he showed her his anger. What good would shouting do?

'I said—do up your belt!'

She grabbed for the handhold on the door. 'I can't do it up when you're lurching around like this!'

He stopped so suddenly that she almost went through the windscreen. She stared at him and he glared back.

'Do it up.'

'All right,' she muttered. 'But I'm damned if I'm letting you go on treating me like this.' She didn't know where the anger came from, but it was here, hot and comforting. 'If there's some point to this circus ride, you can tell me, can't you? Otherwise, I want to go back home.'

Home. She flinched as she heard the word escape her lips.

'We're going to the upper field,' he said grimly.

She wasn't going to be the first to look away. She wasn't going to be pushed out of his life either. Not like this. If he thought he could get away with this, he'd find out he was wrong.

'Why?' she asked. 'Why are we going up there?'

The muscle in his jaw jerked, the only sign that the frozen mask of his face covered something else. 'We're going to talk,' he said grimly.

'Oh.' She leaned back in her seat. 'Fine. It's time we talked.'

Her heart was thundering. If only she could keep this anger alive. It gave her courage and she was going to need courage. He started the truck again and drove up the hill at a more reasonable pace, but it was a rough ride even at slow speed. Faith hung on to the handhold and tried to think what she would say to him when they got up there. What was he planning to tell her? If he offered her alimony or whatever it was a man offered when the marriage was annulled, she'd have no trouble keeping her anger in full flow.

How dared he think he could pay her off?

The winding road twisted up to tall cedars and pine trees. When they crested the hill, Max stopped the truck. She looked ahead through the windscreen, afraid to turn and see what might be in his face.

The world was laid out below them. Slowly, Faith opened her door and got out of the truck. The house was below, and the rolling green hills that sloped down to the thread that was the river. She walked towards the cliff.

'This is how it looked from the plane,' she whispered.

'Get back from that cliff. If you fall...'

She turned and he was standing half a metre away, his hand stretched as if to pull her back. 'If I fell you'd be rid of me,' she said in a flat voice. 'Isn't that what you want?'

Something flashed in his eyes. Pain. As if it hurt for him to think of her gone.

She felt the heat of the sun on her head, heard the insects buzzing near by. Was it possible that he did not want her to leave?

'We can't go on like this,' he said.

'No,' she agreed.

He grabbed her arm and pulled her away from the cliff.

Had he brought her up here to say goodbye?

'I'm not going to lie,' she said huskily.

His fingers tightened on the inside of her elbow. 'What lie are you talking about this time?'

'I've never lied to you.' She pulled away from him and stared down at the short grass growing under a pine tree. 'There are things I haven't told you, but I've never lied.' She met his eyes and said the words. 'I'm not going to disappear from your life and pretend we were never married. I'm not going to do it. I'm not pretending that...' She felt the heat in her face and made herself go on. 'I won't pretend our marriage wasn't consummated and—and—I'm not going to let you dump me on Juan and send me back home. And if you... if you try to divorce me I'll... I'll fight you.'

She turned away, afraid of what would be in his eyes. She took a few paces to the big cedar tree. She traced the rough bark with her fingers. Why didn't he say something? The bark was flaking off in grey strands. She breathed in the smell of his world. Cedar and pine. She was not going to leave. Somehow...

She turned and leaned against the tree, needing its support and hope the weakness in her legs would not show.

'We can't go on the way we are, Faith.'

'No. I know.' She closed her eyes. No tears. The last time she'd cried, he had walked away from her.

He came towards her like the cougar they had seen stalking through the mountain grass last week. 'No lies, Faith.'

'No,' she whispered. 'But what will make you believe my truth?'

His eyes were locked on her face with an intensity that made her bite her lip. 'You said there were things you hadn't told me?'

'Yes.'

'Tell me now.'

She sucked in a jagged breath. 'You already think so badly of me.'

His eyes told her nothing except that he was waiting.

She hugged herself, staring past him at the valley below. 'I was terrified in that plane, coming from Vancouver. A little plane and it was all nightmares. Memories.' She jerked her gaze away from the valley, found his face shuttered and harsh. She gulped and said, 'It was a crash. I didn't tell you it was a plane crash. A little place in the Andes. And I... and I...'

She put out her hands to ward him off because he was coming closer and his arms were stretched out to touch her.

'Don't!' she begged. 'If you touch me I'll cry and you hate it when I cry. I was the only one who survived the crash and... and——'

'You were in the crash that killed Alan? That's when you lost the baby?'

'Yes.'

'You could have told me.' He cursed softly. 'We could have driven. Hell! We could have taken the *train* up from Mexico.'

'It wasn't as bad as I thought it would be. I—I trusted you not to crash us and I can't just give in to being afraid.' She sucked in a big lungful of air and said on a rush, 'I can leave if you don't want me here, but I'm not going back to Peru.' She would stay in the village, or somewhere closer to the ranch if she could. She would find a job. Wayne had been talking about getting a housekeeper to help Beth now that the baby had come, and Beth would want Faith if she offered. Beth would want to help Faith fight for Max's love.

'Is that what you want?' he demanded harshly. 'Do you want to leave?'

She stared back at him, unable to answer.

A muscle jerked in his throat. 'We did this all wrong.'

'Did we?'

He shoved his hands through his hair. He muttered a curse and she felt the last thread of hope tearing inside her.

'I'll leave,' she said. 'Today.'

He spun back to her, coming towards her with something in his face that made her jump back. 'If you leave, I'll follow you. You'd save a lot by staying.'

The look on his face... She'd seen it once before, in the light of dawn, Max staring down at her with the musky smell of loving all around them and pain in his eyes.

'You don't want me,' she whispered painfully. 'I saw how you looked after we—after—and you didn't want—you wished me anywhere but in...in your bed. That time—in the dawn. I saw your eyes.'

His jaw jutted out. 'I wanted to make you say my name. I touched you and you closed your eyes and I knew you were pretending it was your husband touching you.'

She gasped and he paced away from her, his boots sharp on the ground, an angry echo of his voice. 'I promised myself I wouldn't touch you,' he growled. 'That I'd never touch you until it was me in your eyes.' The breath went out of him in jerks and his voice turned flat. 'Then I made a hell of a mistake,' he said painfully. 'The other day, when you had the baby in our bedroom.'

Our bedroom. As if in his heart that was how he wanted them to be. Together. Man and wife.

'A mistake?' she whispered.

He threw his head back. 'I succeeded in making you cry. That's all. And I proved it wasn't me you wanted.' His eyes were bleak, his face stone. 'I'd told myself that I could ask and you would cry out *my* name, but I saw your tears and I knew why you were crying.'

She tried to move, but the trembling inside was so deep she could hardly speak. 'Because I wanted——'

'You wanted your husband.'

She whispered. '*You* are my husband. You are the only man...'

'One day, I will be. I promise you that. The next time I touch you, there will be no one in your heart but me.'

She reached then, towards him, but he stepped back, shaking his head sharply.

'Maybe we started this thing as a business deal, your body in my bed for my...' The breath went out of him and he growled, 'That's not how it's going to go on. If you're staying—I want it all, Faith.'

'I'm staying,' she promised in a voice that was husky.

'Then I'm sleeping in the guest room.'

His eyes were telling her that the last place he wanted to be was in the guest room. 'And then?' she asked breathlessly. 'Will you stay there forever?'

His gaze took hers for a long, sober moment. 'And then I'm going to begin courting you.'

'How long does courting take?' she asked breathlessly.

'Until there's only one man in your heart.'

'And then...you'll move back...into...into our room?' She saw what was in his eyes. She did now know when it had happened, but it was love in his eyes. 'I thought you brought me up on this mountain to send me away. I—I thought—I was afraid——'

His sharp negative told her more than he knew. 'I promised you a child,' he said. 'And I'll deliver, but first...' He was smiling slightly now and his voice had turned husky and harsh mixed together. 'I want you and I'm going to win you. I can accept that you loved your husband, but he's gone and I'm here. And one day you'll look at me and I'll be the only man you could ever want.

The only man you love. I promise you that day will come.'

She could hardly hear his words over the sound of her heart. He jerked his head in warning when she took a step towards him.

'There's more that I didn't tell you.' Her voice was stronger now.

'Then tell me.'

She took two steps before his eyes warned her to stop.

'Don't touch me, Faith. Not until you mean it. You're very good at driving me mad, but the next time I——'

'I'll tell you everything. She moved closer still and his chest was hard with tight muscles. She touched and felt the jerk of his flesh, the answering awareness inside herself. 'You thought from the beginning that I was still mourning Alan. You thought that when we made love...'

She realised that she was staring at her own hand on his chest and lifted her eyes, because some things had to be said straight from her heart to his. 'I should have told you the truth, but—you thought badly of me already. If I was mourning my marriage to Alan, it was because it never was a real marriage. I was very young when I met him—nineteen—and I fell in love...' She placed her other hand on his chest too. His heart was pounding against her touch.

'Say it,' he ground out. She looked down and his hands were clenched at his sides. Then she looked up and there was fire in his eyes.

'I'm glad you brought me up here,' she said huskily. They would make love here and the trees would see, and the sky.

'Faith, get this over with.' His eyes were shuttered, but she had seen the emotion he tried to hide. 'Say it now, because I don't want to hear his name on your lips again. If you——'

She touched his mouth and his words dried to nothing. 'I have never felt for anyone what I feel for you. Even that first day... Cathy sent me to the island, yes, but there was no plot, no deliberate plan. She didn't know you'd be there, although I did think she'd set me up at first. But when I saw you—when I...'

'Faith...'

She shook her head and the tears were in her throat, but she smiled and her voice was soft with tears and sincerity. 'I thought I loved Alan once, but by the time we'd been married a week, I knew he wasn't the man I'd fallen in love with. Puppy love. Infatuation. For him—he just wanted a connection with the Corsicas. He married me to get a factory in Peru. Not for love. It was ten years with Alan that taught me the acting skills you hate so much in me.'

She lifted her head and found his eyes molten, felt his hands harden on her back.

'I learned to smile at my guests when my husband was having an affair with the maid. If there had been a child I would have buried myself in the child. It's as well there wasn't.' She sucked in a deep breath. 'And I'm glad I'm not pregnant now, because there'd be no other way for me to prove it's you I love. Until I fell in love with you I never realised what love was. I do want a child and I've dreamed that you and I could—that our child would help you love me.'

'Faith...hush.' He was going to kiss her, but she stopped him with her fingers against his mouth. She swallowed twice and went on softly, her eyes on his.

'There's never been anyone but you in my heart. If you don't believe me... It isn't just because I want a child. I—we can practise birth control. I'd—I'd give up anything to be with you.' Her fingers hardened and pressed against his lips. 'But if you ever look at another woman—don't think I'll stand for it. I'd kill her.'

'You crazy fool! Don't you know I could never look at another woman?' He held her away slightly so that he could look into her eyes. What she saw in his face made her flesh flame. He pulled her against him. 'You should blush, you witch. When you touch me—you know exactly what your touch does, don't you?'

'Yes,' she admitted. Her hands moved on his chest and she felt him tense. She slid her hand down against his midriff and his face darkened with a deep flush. 'I thought it was my only weapon to win you,' she said soberly.

He took her face in his hands. 'Why did you cry the last time I began to make love to you?' He was staring down into her eyes, and she knew that he could see the tears collecting again, because his lips turned down into a frown.

'Loving you, I ached for you to touch me, to love me. But it was hate in your eyes and when I—I wanted to cry out, to beg you to... to love me, please to love me—and I... your face was so hard and...' She shuddered. 'I could see your regret, that you wished you'd never married me, never let me get into your life.'

His hands caressed her shoulders, warm and hard, an echo of his voice. 'I wanted to love you from the first, but I told myself I'd be crazy to go along with your marriage proposal. But when you were walking away back on Isla Catalina—I couldn't let you go.' He bent to take her lips in a hard kiss. 'I simply could not let you walk away. I knew it would take time if we were going to make anything of our marriage. I told myself—I hated myself when I took you on our wedding night.'

'I was afraid you didn't want me,' she whispered.

'How the hell could I take advantage of your love for a dead man? But then I did, and I couldn't stop myself from coming back to your bed again and again. Whenever I thought you were going to say his name——' his eyes turned bleak '—I covered your mouth with mine to silence you. I wanted to watch you when I heard the breathless sounds you made, but I didn't dare. If you had looked into my eyes and I'd seen disappointment because I wasn't him... if you had whispered his name when I was inside you...'

She slid her hands up around his neck, into his hair. 'You were wrong. You have to believe that. Love me now. Here... please, Max.'

She touched him and he groaned and his lips came down on hers and she tried to say her love, but she was spinning... dying... and he was the world and the sun and his hands were running up and down her back and then he was touching her inside the big, loose sweater. She felt herself sag against him and he lifted his head and her eyes were glazed and half closed and she reached again for his lips.

'If you let go of me I'll fall,' she warned him as she pressed her mouth to his. 'And if you kiss me like that again...'

'I love you,' he said soberly, his eyes on hers. 'I've never loved any woman the way I love you.'

'I dreamed you would.' Her voice was only a whisper. 'Max...my love...I've been waiting for you all my life.' She wound her arms around his neck and pulled herself close, and his hands ran up her bare back inside the sweater and found no barrier but her flesh.

He bent his head and buried his face against her throat. His hands slid around to possess her breasts and a broken cry of desire was torn from her throat. 'For me?' he asked huskily. 'Trying to tempt me?'

'Yes,' she admitted. She had left the bra off when she'd dressed to go down to the paddock, something she never did. 'I—I had no other way to try to change your mind. I thought—maybe you still wanted me. But—I was going to wear the red flannel shirt, but I got scared at the last minute and this sweater is such a bulky knit...'

He swept the sweater away and she was standing in the sun, her heart pounding at the look in his eyes. He bent and kissed her breasts and she moaned as a knife of sensation struck to the centre of her.

'Please,' she begged.

He swept her up into his arms. She was held high, safe. She cupped his cheek with her hand, closed her eyes as he bent his head to kiss her again.

'Beautiful,' he murmured in a shaken voice. 'Oh, God, darling! It's been so long and I don't want to wait any longer, but it's all pine needles here and I've only got my shirt to protect you.'

'Please,' she whispered. She drew her thumb across the nub of his male nipple, then buried her face in his throat as he lowered her to the ground and took his shirt off. She helped him, her heart racing with passion when her touch made his fingers fumble and his eyes darken with need. Her hand moved to his buckle.

'Lady, if you're going to undress me...' He fumbled with her jeans fastener and then his palm was flat on her belly and she could feel her pulse beating there and when he moved her world spun to nothing but the roaring of her own pulse.

She tried to speak, but he was drawing her jeans away from her, touching her in ways he knew would send her mad with need. She groaned, 'Oh, Max, if you stop...'

He moved his lips to hers and took her mouth in a kiss that was only a parody of the possession they both needed. 'Does it feel as if I'm stopping?' he asked in a voice that was as shaken as her pulse.

'If—if you want us to practice birth control...I...oh, Max! If you...please! Oh, please! I love you so much! I can't stand——'

He moved over her and brushed her lips gently with his own. 'Yes, you can.' His body moved against hers and she moaned and moved in the rhythm of loving.

'You're my wife, Faith Davidson.' His voice was shaken with emotion as he promised her, 'I'm going to enjoy giving you my child...our child.'

When he lifted his head, his eyes caressed her lips. Then he looked deep into her eyes and saw all he would ever need there. 'You've nothing to prove to me, darling,' he said in a deep voice that made her heart swell. 'Just let me show you how much I love you.'

'Yes,' she whispered. 'Forever...I love you.'

He took her then, high on the hill above the home where their children would grow surrounded by their love.

MILLS & BOON

EXCITING NEW COVERS

The Baby Contract
SUZANNE CAREY

Tender Assault
ANNE MATHER

To reflect the ever-changing contemporary romance series we've designed new covers which perfectly capture the warmth, glamour and sophistication of modern-day romantic situations.

We know, because we've designed them with your comments in mind, that you'll just love the bright, warm, romantic colours and the up-to-date new look.

WATCH OUT FOR THESE NEW COVERS

From October 1993   Price £1.80

Available from W.H. Smith, John Menzies, Martins, Forbuoys, most supermarkets and other paperback stockists.
Also available from Mills & Boon Reader Service, Freepost, PO Box 236, Thornton Road, Croydon, Surrey CR9 9EL. (UK Postage & Packing free)

THREE SENSUOUS STORIES...

ONE BEAUTIFUL VOLUME

A special collection of three individual love stories, beautifully presented in one absorbing volume.

One of the world's most popular romance authors, Charlotte Lamb has written over 90 novels, including the bestselling *Barbary Wharf* six part mini-series. This unique edition features three of her earlier titles, together for the first time in one collectable volume.

AVAILABLE FROM SEPTEMBER 1993   PRICED £4.99

W❶RLDWIDE

Available from W. H. Smith, John Menzies, Martins, Forbuoys, most supermarkets and other paperback stockists.
Also available from Worldwide Reader Service, FREEPOST, PO Box 236, Thornton Road, Croydon, Surrey CR9 9EL. (UK Postage & Packing free)

4 FREE

Romances and 2 FREE gifts just for you!

You can enjoy all the heartwarming emotion of true love for FREE! Discover the heartbreak and happiness, the emotion and the tenderness of the modern relationships in Mills & Boon Romances.

We'll send you 4 Romances as a special offer from Mills & Boon Reader Service, along with the opportunity to have 6 captivating new Romances delivered to your door each month.

Claim your FREE books and gifts overleaf...

An irresistible offer from Mills & Boon

Become a regular reader of Romances with Mills & Boon Reader Service and we'll welcome you with 4 books, a CUDDLY TEDDY and a special MYSTERY GIFT all absolutely FREE.

And then look forward to receiving 6 brand new Romances each month, delivered to your door hot off the presses, postage and packing FREE! Plus our free Newsletter featuring author news, competitions, special offers and much more.

This invitation comes with no strings attached. You may cancel or suspend your subscription at any time, and still keep your free books and gifts.

It's so easy. Send no money now. Simply fill in the coupon below and post it to -
Reader Service, FREEPOST, PO Box 236, Croydon, Surrey CR9 9EL.

NO STAMP REQUIRED

Free Books Coupon

Yes! Please rush me 4 FREE Romances and 2 FREE gifts! Please also reserve me a Reader Service subscription. If I decide to subscribe I can look forward to receiving 6 brand new Romances for just £10.80 each month, postage and packing FREE. If I decide not to subscribe I shall write to you within 10 days - I can keep the free books and gifts whatever I choose. I may cancel or suspend my subscription at any time. I am over 18 years of age.

Ms/Mrs/Miss/Mr _____ EP56R

Address _____

_____

Postcode _____ Signature _____

Offers closes 31st March 1994. The right is reserved to refuse an application and change the terms of this offer. This offer does not apply to Romance subscribers. One application per household. Overseas readers please write for details. Southern Africa write to Book Services International Ltd., Box 41654, Craighall, Transvaal 2024. You may be mailed with offers from other reputable companies as a result of this application. Please tick box if you would prefer not to receive such offers. ☐

mps MAILING PREFERENCE SERVICE

TORN BETWEEN TWO WORLDS...

A delicate Eurasian beauty who moved between two worlds, but was shunned by both. An innocent whose unawakened fires could be ignited by only one man. This sensuous tale sweeps from remotest China to the decadence of old Shanghai, reaching its heart-stirring conclusion in the opulent Longwarden mansion and lush estates of Edwardian England.

Available now priced £3.99

WORLDWIDE

*Available from W. H. Smith, John Menzies, Martins, Forbuoys, most supermarkets and other paperback stockists.
Also available from Worldwide Reader Service, FREEPOST, PO Box 236, Thornton Road, Croydon, Surrey CR9 9EL. (UK Postage & Packing free)*

Next Month's Romances

Each month you can choose from a wide variety of romance with Mills & Boon. Below are the new titles to look out for next month, why not ask either Mills & Boon Reader Service or your Newsagent to reserve you a copy of the titles you want to buy – just tick the titles you would like and either post to Reader Service or take it to any Newsagent and ask them to order your books.

Please save me the following titles:		Please tick	√
A DIFFICULT MAN	Lindsay Armstrong		
MARRIAGE IN JEOPARDY	Miranda Lee		
TENDER ASSAULT	Anne Mather		
RETURN ENGAGEMENT	Carole Mortimer		
LEGACY OF SHAME	Diana Hamilton		
A PART OF HEAVEN	Jessica Marchant		
CALYPSO'S ISLAND	Rosalie Ash		
CATCH ME IF YOU CAN	Anne McAllister		
NO NEED FOR LOVE	Sandra Marton		
THE FABERGE CAT	Anne Weale		
AND THE BRIDE WORE BLACK	Helen Brooks		
LOVE IS THE ANSWER	Jennifer Taylor		
BITTER POSSESSION	Jenny Cartwright		
INSTANT FIRE	Liz Fielding		
THE BABY CONTRACT	Suzanne Carey		
NO TRESPASSING	Shannon Waverly		

If you would like to order these books in addition to your regular subscription from Mills & Boon Reader Service please send £1.80 per title to: Mills & Boon Reader Service, Freepost, P.O. Box 236, Croydon, Surrey, CR9 9EL, quote your Subscriber No:................................... (If applicable) and complete the name and address details below. Alternatively, these books are available from many local Newsagents including W.H.Smith, J.Menzies, Martins and other paperback stockists from 8 October 1993.

Name:..
Address:..
....Post Code:.........................

To Retailer: If you would like to stock M&B books please contact your regular book/magazine wholesaler for details.

You may be mailed with offers from other reputable companies as a result of this application.
If you would rather not take advantage of these opportunities please tick box ☐